Sobekkare's Revenge

Angela Dorsey

Sobekkare's Revenge

Cover layout: Stabenfeldt A/S
Typeset by Roberta L. Melzl
Edited by Bobbie Chase
Printed in Germany 2006

ISBN: 1-933343-27-3

Stabenfeldt, Inc.
457 North Main Street
Danbury, CT 06811
www.pony.us

The first strange thing Sobekkare noticed was a tiny breath of wind against her shoulder. It amazed her to feel it in this land where wind did not exist. She looked to her right, but saw only the usual gray sands stretching away into infinity.

Her dark thoughts distracted her and she leaned forward on her throne to watch the soldiers before her. Their shouts saturated the air and swords clanged and clashed: a perfect dissonance of hatred. Yes, her army was winning. Again.

Then she heard a whisper – and it wasn't from her realm either. With this battle raging about her, it would be impossible to hear a whisper from her own kingdom. No, this was a whisper from the other place. Slowly, Sobekkare straightened on her throne. She'd almost forgotten what voices sounded like in that far away land, it was so long since she'd heard them. Centuries. But there was no mistaking it: the soft voice, full of excitement and joy and wonderment.

Had someone finally come for her treasure? And in doing so, had they at last opened the door to her revenge?

There was no other explanation. A sudden explosion of anticipation thrummed through her veins, and she felt like a lioness that has been caged for eons and is finally freed! Now she could wreak her vengeance! At last! At last!

She drew in a trembling breath and closed her eyes to further concentrate on the lush, wild exultation of being unbound, and discovered to her amazement that she could see in that other place! The view was limited, for she was looking through the eyes of her rage – and therefore through the eyes of the onyx, Enemy-shaped figurine: that object into which

she'd directed all the incredible fury she felt for the Enemies. But still, she could see, and that was what mattered.

A man was reaching toward her to pick her up, or rather, toward the black stone statuette she saw through. Soon she would be free! She would be loosed upon all Enemies, ripping at their minds, tearing into their sanity, and turning them toward madness. She would destroy them! What tremendous satisfaction, her revenge just moments away!

Abruptly, the man dropped her and Sobekkare looked up to see revulsion in his expression. He felt my anger, she realized in horror. Oh no! Have I lost my chance? I must control myself until I am freed, until this man carries me from the tomb and the light of day touches the onyx figurine. Then nothing can stop me!

She stuffed down her ferocity as best she could and watched, impatiently, as the man moved on to rifle through the treasures that, centuries before, had belonged to her. He selected this one and that, placed them carefully into canvas sacks, and carried them to the back door of her tomb. After lowering the treasures down the cliff, he returned to select more, and then more, and more. And every time he walked past her without a sideways glance.

When he came back the sixth time, Sobekkare sensed finality in his walk. The man looked exhausted. Was he almost finished?

Her fears were right. When the sacks were full this time, the man picked up his lantern and left.

Take me, take me, she roared silently as he walked past her for the last time. And he stopped, bent, reached. Sobekkare's heart raced, and in her kingdom she smiled. He was going to pick up the statuette and take her from the tomb. He was going to free her rage!

But the man's hand moved too far and he overreached the stone Enemy-shaped carving to pick up Sobekkare's evening crown. He stuffed the elegant, ruby-studded diadem into the sack and turned away.

Please, take me too! She begged silently, and rued her voiceless form in this world. Rued the fact she'd been reduced to begging – and she a queen! But he must take her, she must have her revenge, and if begging would help, she would do it. Please. Don't leave me here to wait for another thousand years!

The man was almost at the back door now, his lantern swinging jauntily in his hand. He was leaving, and happy to do so.

Please. Please!

The man was at the slit in the rock wall now.

Please…

And he turned, and looked back toward her dark form on the floor. "Aisha," he whispered. Then he set the lantern down and walked back toward her. He bent and touched the onyx Enemy with one fingertip, testing it. Sobekkare sucked in her emotion as much as she could, hiding her rage behind polite masks. She was half aware that even her soldiers in her kingdom were quieting. She tried to think of gardens and flowers and sparkling pools, of beautiful dresses and crowns and jewels. How happy she'd been back then, before the Enemies – but she couldn't think of them. He would feel her anger.

Success! He was picking her up! He was placing her in the sack! He was carrying her toward the door.

And then she was outside, and being lowered down the cliff. The evening breeze swept through the drawstring opening, tempting her, beckoning to her, and she felt herself rise on the wind – to discover she had been freed too late to wreak her vengeance this day. The sun had set, though barely. But Sobekkare did not despair. Soon the sun would rise again. And besides, now that she was released from the tomb, she felt a little stronger in this world. She moved a short distance from her host, the Enemy figurine, and invisibly circled the sack as the man lowered it to the wadi floor.

The wadi was much the same as she remembered it: small, narrow, and insignificant. How she hated that her burial tomb was here instead of in a vast majestic pyramid. Her rage swept back in a rush. It was the fault of the Shepherd Kings and the Enemies! They'd come to her beautiful world and stolen her

8

land and her people. They'd pretended to be her friends and then ripped her life apart, turning her into an outcast and a fugitive in her own land.

If she'd fought only the Shepherd Kings' armies, she would have repelled the invaders. Hadn't she proven that in her recreated battles, again and again?

But the Shepherd Kings had brought the strange Enemies with them – wild maned creatures with dark, glistening eyes and hooves of iron. And Sobekkare's soldiers had fled before them, terrified beyond reason of the terrible fiends.

There! Right below her! Sobekkare could hardly believe her eyes. One of the Enemies was here in her wadi! She strained toward the creature, her rage pounding like a drum in her brain. She couldn't wait for dawn to start the destruction. Though the sun hadn't yet touched the onyx Enemy figurine, her hatred gave her some power. On this night, she would make the first Enemy start suffering for the years of torment she'd endured – as much as she was able, anyway.

Sobekkare was amazed and even a little awed at the destructive force of her fury. Her first victim seemed very susceptible to the dark visions she forced into its mind – monsters creeping through darkness, ready to consume it; boulders falling from the sky to crush it; the ground beneath its feet turning to mush and sucking it down, down, down.

Terror flowed from it, and calmly, steadily, and with great satisfaction, Sobekkare sucked the Enemy's terror-energy into the onyx statuette, into herself. Her power in this realm was growing by the moment, her influence was becoming stronger. And now she felt powerful enough to cast her web even wider.

And she found even more Enemies only a few miles away! What had they been doing over the last thousand years? Conquering the entire world?

Well, she would stop them and their evil ways! Their reign of terror was at an end! Their nemesis, Queen Sobekkare, had returned!

Abdullah was so exhausted he could hardly stand, yet he knew he wouldn't sleep this night either. Excitement still roared like liquid fire through his veins. He'd never known anything like it.

He'd spent the last hours excavating the ancient tomb he'd discovered, pulling artifact after priceless artifact from the depths of history and lowering them carefully down the treacherous cliff. Then, when he knew his camels would be unable to carry more, he reluctantly left the fortune that remained, resealed the tomb, and camouflaged the tomb's back door, a mere slit in the rock face barely wide enough to squeeze through. Finally, when he felt confident that no other treasure hunters would discover the tomb, he cautiously climbed down the cliff.

There was only one thing more to do before he left: pack the beautifully jeweled cups, necklaces, headdresses, scarabs, and figurines into the camels' dusty packs. Thrills raced through him as he inspected each piece by the light of the small fire he'd built. How incredibly fortunate he was! He still had difficulty believing he'd discovered a thousand-year-old burial site in this unremarkable wadi. But it had happened, and these treasures were the proof. He picked up a golden amulet, positive it was the prettiest item of the bunch. He changed his mind when a lapis lazuli studded tiara caught his eye. Nothing could be lovelier. How wonderful it would look on his wife's raven black hair.

This onyx horse would be the perfect gift for his youngest child, Aisha, and Abdullah was glad he'd gone back to pick it up again. It was silly to think an artifact carried a negative feeling. He was too tired, that's all. And Aisha would love this artifact even more than the ones glittering with precious stones. He'd never understood his daughter's fascination with horses, but the entire family had soon learned to watch the toddler all the time. She would run to any horse, old or young, trained or not, and throw her arms around one of its legs as if embracing a long lost grandmother. In fact, he'd felt terrible when he told her he was taking Bastet with him for a few weeks. His young daughter's eyes had filled with tears and her cheeks, for once not dimpled into a smile, said more to him than words ever could. This gift, however, this precious onyx horse, would make it up to her. Smiling, he wrapped the black stone carving in linen and laid it inside the pack with the other treasures.

A few feet away, Bastet's hoof struck the ground. Once. Twice. Abdullah didn't look up.

His sons, what would they chose? The older boy would probably like the short sword. He was the adventurer. And the younger, the scholar, might choose some of the richly housed papyrus scrolls. Abdullah smiled again. It seemed so bizarre. Just yesterday morning, he'd been a destitute man, and he and his family had few prospects. Now they were rich beyond their wildest imaginations!

What would his wife say when he showed her the treasures? Probably nothing for the first few minutes – she would be speechless with joy! She would know what his discovery would mean to their family, to her mother who was ill, to their children's futures, to their standard of living. They would live in luxury for years now, as he slowly sold most of the artifacts to the dealers. And if they spent all their money, he would return to the tomb and bring out the rest of the treasure. There was enough inside still to last a lifetime, and beyond!

Bastet neighed loudly and Abdullah started. The horse pawed the ground again and snorted. The whites of her eyes glistening in the light of his fire reminded him that he'd have to douse the fire before he left. And he still had to hide the gear he was leaving behind. If he didn't stop daydreaming and get busy, he'd never get on his way, or get home to tell his wife of their vast good fortune, or give his children their magnificent gifts. Just a few more items to put in the packs and he was almost ready to start the long journey home – and the knowledge that he was riding toward a new and privileged life would keep his exhaustion at bay. Or so he hoped.

Nefret, my beauty, it is I, Angelica. My dear Aswan, try not to be anxious. I will do my best to help you both. Please, as I regain my strength, tell me what is wrong. I can feel your fear, and can tell it is more than a simple fear. It is closer to a deep and paralyzing horror. What is amiss? What has happened?

You do not know what is wrong? You do not know why you are afraid? But I do not understand. How can you not know? There must be a reason for your terror.

Yet suddenly, I too feel immobilized by strange horrors. I cannot seem to clear my head. Your baseless fear is infecting me as well. Dread has stolen into my mind and is warping my thoughts, turning them toward... what? Madness? What a strange and ghastly sensation this is, creeping into my being!

Finally, I can see. There are dark buildings through the stable door, and the stars above them, too dim. The moon appears to have a veil drawn across it, muting its luminous glory. Yet I know the moon has not changed. This terror is affecting my sight as well.

Stand firm, Nefret and Aswan. I must put a spirit barrier between us. Only then will I be able to think clearly and discover what is happening here. I am sorry to leave you alone in your fear for these few moments, but I must if I am to understand.

Ah, I can sense it now. Something is reaching for you: a power, both ancient and malignant, a dark hand of freezing horror. It is attempting to steal your life force. It is attempting to destroy you. Such hatred! Such loathing!

And why?

My loves, I will remove the barrier between us, and then we must go. We must journey to the source of the evil and discover the why of it, if we hope to stop it. Be brave, my dears, and hurry, before the terror within our hearts grows too strong!

Jumana sat up in bed, instantly wide-awake, wide-eyed, and anxious. She looked around the room she shared with her younger sister, Laila. Even without a light, she could tell nothing was wrong. The white walls gleamed in the moonlight, bare and featureless. Her sister lay in the bed beside her, her breathing calm and steady. So what was this strange disquiet Jumana felt? What had awakened her? Had she heard something? Was it an unremembered dream?

"Laila?" she whispered.

The six-year-old didn't stir. A slight movement caught Jumana's eye and she raised her eyes to the open window above their bed. Outside, palms swayed in a slight breeze, their fronds rattling quietly against each other. The delicate wind reached in to caress Jumana's cheek and she closed her eyes to feel the wind on her eyelids. It seemed a perfectly ordinary night. So what was this peculiar unease she felt?

Maybe it's Nefret! she thought, and her eyes sprung open. *What if she and Aswan are sick?* She'd overheard her father telling her mother that the horses were acting nervous that evening. *But he didn't sound overly worried about them, and he knows a lot about horses*, she reminded herself, then smiled into the darkness. *However, it's the perfect opportunity to go visit Nefret!* She'd been so busy helping her mother all day that she hadn't had time to spend with the mare.

Moving as carefully as possible so as not to wake Laila, she slid from beneath their light blankets. Her sister inhaled sharply and Jumana caught her breath, expecting Laila to open her eyes. Instead, the little girl rolled over to face the wall and her breathing became rhythmic once more.

Once Jumana closed the front door behind her, a surge of exhilaration swept through her body making her pulse race. She felt so free! Moments alone and unfettered were few and far between. Her days were so full of work and school, do this and do that, that time to spend as she pleased, unwatched and without chores to do, felt wonderful. Not that she blamed her parents for her hectic life. They worked much harder than she did. They weren't a rich family and with Jumana, Laila, and their two baby brothers, Umar and Alem, to care for, her parents seemed to be running from one chore to another all the time.

She threw her arms wide as she ran across the moonlit courtyard, exalting in the feel of the wind flowing around her. Her hair streamed back like a silky mane. She'd missed her time with Nefret today. The beautiful chestnut mare was like a sister to her, a closer sister than even Laila. Jumana told Nefret things she would never tell anyone else, and the chestnut mare always listened with one ear cocked toward her and dark eyes locked on Jumana's hazel ones. The girl was never sure how much Nefret understood her, but she was convinced the gentle horse comprehended the feelings behind her words, if not their actual meaning.

She reached the stable doorway and leaned inside. The interior was pitch black. "Nefret."

There was no response.

"Nefret?" Why wasn't the elegant mare answering her? Was she asleep? Jumana tried to peer through the stable's darkness, hoping to see Nefret's white star floating in the gloom, but could see nothing.

"Aswan?" Jumana tried, thinking that maybe the steel-gray stallion would answer. She held her breath as she waited for his response, but there was no answering whinny, no hoof stamping on the dirt floor, no swishing of a long tail.

With one hand holding the doorpost, she stepped into the darkness. Carefully, she felt her way toward the horses' tie stalls, found the divider between the two, and stepped inside Nefret's stall. She reached to touch the mare's hindquarters and felt only empty space. Her chest tightened as she stumbled with outstretched arms toward the manger. Nefret's dinner was only half eaten, even though the horses had been fed hours before. Jumana felt for the ring the mare was tied to and discovered the rope still knotted to the iron with the halter hanging from the end of it.

"Oh no," she whispered, her fingers desperately feeling for a break in the leather. But there was no defect. The halter had simply been unfastened. She moved swiftly around the partition and into Aswan's stall to find his halter, undamaged as well, hanging from the ring attached to the wall.

With her breath coming in gasps, Jumana hurried toward the door. Nefret and Aswan had been stolen! She had to get help, and quickly!

Jumana was halfway across the courtyard, sprinting toward the house, when a thought speared into her mind and stopped her short. The moon hung above the horizon in front of her like a pendant ready to fall over the edge of the world. Soon it would be behind the distant hills and the town would be swamped in darkness. Only a few minutes of moonlight remained in which to spot the thief escaping with Aswan and Nefret, and she needed to know which direction he was taking them. If she couldn't tell her parents where he was headed, there would hardly be a point in waking them. They wouldn't know which way to go to recover the horses until dawn touched the eastern sky, many hours from now, and the thief would have a massive head start by then.

She turned and ran toward the center of the village, straight toward the mosque. She couldn't wait for dawn to pursue the thief. There was too good a chance he'd get away.

The building glistened before her in the subtle light, and the minaret towered upward from its bulk, shining the brightest of all. The minaret was the highest point in the village by far, and from its tower windows she could see not only the entire village but beyond, into the desert. She'd find them, unless they were hiding in the moon shadows of some building. Or unless the moon set before she could locate them. Or unless they were already miles away, far beyond the range of her vision. Lost to her forever.

Stop! Stop here beside this building. I am being called away. More voices are suddenly clamoring for help. All are confused and fearful. All are terror filled. They are as frightened as you are, my dear Aswan and Nefret. The same terrible malady afflicts you all.

But before I go, there is something I must do. I must connect to you in the ancient way of horses and guardians past. Hold still, my Aswan. To you I will connect first. And now you, my dear Nefret.

It is done. And now, I can lend you my strength, even when I am not beside you. My energy can be a shield against the worst of the terrors that run through your mind.

Now I must go to the others, one by one, and connect to them as I did to you, so I may hold you all safe in my heart and mind and soul, for as long as I possibly can.

And my dears, you must carry on alone toward our goal, the source of this evil. You must follow this most horrid of feelings to its strongest point, to its beginning place. You must go where you most fear to go.

I will return to you as soon as I can.

Now to whom shall I go first? Who is in the direst need?

By the time she reached the mosque, Jumana's side ached and her breath was coming in gasps. She slumped against the wall for a moment, her hand clutching her ribs, then pushed on the heavy door. Within moments, she was pounding up the stairs inside the minaret. The sound of her footsteps echoed around and around her as she climbed upward, upward, upward through the darkness.

Finally she reached the windows, one facing each direction. She leaned on the railing and peered down onto the village below, her eyes searching the shadows and crevices. The moonlight shone bright on the buildings and courtyards, the marketplace and streets. Slowly, she raised her eyes and searched the houses and stables, the schoolhouse, and now the open desert, her breath still coming quickly, her heart racing. No movement caught her eye so she methodically moved to the next window and began again. Still nothing. And then the third window. Her gaze snagged on dark forms here and there and she watched each for a few seconds. When they didn't move, her gaze swept onward. Then the fourth window. And still nothing.

But they had to be there! She just wasn't seeing them, that's all. She had to keep trying. Maybe they were in the shadow of one of the buildings. Maybe they hadn't yet made their way to the open desert where they would be more visible. She refused to think the other thought that kept trying to intrude – that they were long gone, too far away to see at all.

At the end of her second full circle, she was almost ready to give up. And she was running out of time! The moon balanced on the peak for a breathless moment, and then started its inevitable plunge behind the dry black mountain. Within three minutes, it would be gone. She had mere moments to spot them now. She peered into the night, desperate. They had to be there somewhere.

She caught a movement out of the corner of her eye, two dark shapes moving out from the moon shadow of the clinic at the edge of the village. There they were! But the two forms didn't look as she'd expected. She peered through the last of the moonshine, trying to see them more clearly. Could it be her imagination? In this meager light, was she seeing what was really there? Because, honestly, she couldn't see a rider on either horse.

Then the moon was down.

Jumana peered over the railing for another moment, then spun around and hurried down the stairs as quickly as she could. The tower was pitch black inside and she held a hand out on either side of her, pressing hard against the walls of the narrow staircase in order to keep her balance. Her mind raced as she descended. If neither horse had a rider, that meant they weren't being stolen. Maybe someone simply set them free as a joke, or as revenge for some imagined slight. Or maybe someone tried to steal them, but they'd escaped. But whatever the reason, the horses were now wandering loose. This new development meant there was no need to wake her parents or disturb anyone's rest. Jumana could catch them herself and bring them home.

Something was wrong. She felt it with the first two she'd found in the Enemy gathering place: a barrier of sorts that blocked her most terrifying visions.

On second thought, it didn't seem like a true barrier. Instead, it seemed as if something between her and the Enemies was absorbing the visions, taking them into itself. Revulsion choked in her throat. Something or someone was there, trying to protect the Enemies. How could they? Didn't they know the Enemies were evil?

Thankfully, there were still unprotected Enemies to target. Sobekkare would concentrate on them, and gain in strength. And when she was strong enough, she would probe the Enemies' protector and destroy it as well.

Ali and Shadi, I am here. Hold still, my loves. Let me draw the connection between us.

Now you, Maysa, and your beautiful foal, Amala. I must say she has been well named. Amala means hope. Her name reminds us to do our best and not despair in this dire situation. Because the terrible visions bring horror and hopelessness, we must all remember Amala – hope – even when our situation seems too difficult.

Now Kalila, my darling one, let me connect to you.

And Zara. Allow me to give you strength.

And now it is done and I must move on. There are others in the village that need me.

Fare well, my loves.

Jumana half walked and half ran down the dark streets away from the mosque. Now that she knew the horses weren't being stolen, she could appreciate her late-night adventure a bit more. The night was so alluring, so magical; it was almost impossible to not linger just a bit. The midnight wind was slight but warm, and brushed against her face as lightly as her mother's hand when Jumana had a fever. The buildings stood firm and strong all along the quiet street, making her feel protected. On the other side of town a dog barked, then silence was reborn, a silence so profound it seemed more significant than any noise.

And the stars! Now that the moon had set, they were brighter than ever. She could see the Milky Way above her, like a radiant cloud in the heavens. To the east, she found the stars in the constellation Pegasus, the flying horse, glowing like diamonds afire in the night sky. Her parents had taught her most of the constellations and Jumana stopped to search a little higher up, a little to the south.

Yes, there it was: Equuleus, the foal, one of the smallest and dimmest constellations in the sky, but still one of her favorites. The image of a graceful foal galloping across the desert beside Nefret and Aswan swept into her mind and she smiled in the darkness. Next year, Nefret should have a foal. How wonderful that would be! A perfect foal to love and train and care for, and with Nefret and Aswan as its parents, she was certain the foal couldn't be anything but wonderful.

But she needed to remember her mission this night. Even though the horses weren't being stolen, they would still be safer inside the village than out on the wild desert. When Nefret and Aswan were beside her, they could linger to enjoy the temptation of the night together. They could take as long as they liked on their way home too. Her family was asleep. No one knew they were gone. They had hours, if they wanted. She was almost to the clinic now. Soon she would be away from the village and reunited with Nefret and Aswan.

A flash of white came from Jumana's right, and automatically she leapt back into the shadows. Brilliant light streamed from the building behind the doctor's house.

The doctor had three fine horses in his stable. Was one of them sick? Was the doctor in there right now, administering to the poor animal?

Almost as suddenly, the light diminished to a gentle flickering glow. Jumana gasped. Without hesitating, she raced toward the doctor's stable. There was only one thing she knew that could cause that pattern of light. Sometimes, if a spark flew from a candle or lantern, it could remain dormant for hours, until it suddenly ignited the stable bedding around it in a burst of brightness. Then it would settle down into a flickering flame that would steadily build to consume everything in its path, including trapped horses!

Jumana sprinted the last few steps. She had to get the horses out before it was too late! There was no time to wake anyone, no time to do anything but untie and lead the doctor's horses from the stable herself. Thank goodness she'd been walking by at that exact moment!

She stopped in the doorway to survey the scene, to decide which of the poor animals was in the most danger, which to run to first – and her mouth dropped open in astonishment.

There was no fire. In fact, there was no flame whatsoever. The light was concentrated in the hands of the palest girl Jumana had ever seen. The girl was standing with her eyes closed, slowly swaying from side to side, as her incandescent fingers spread over the forehead of the doctor's old bay mare, Latif. Her blonde hair swished across her back as she moved, causing sparks to twinkle in the golden floss.

As Jumana watched, breathless, speechless, the radiant tendrils from the girl's hands flowed to surround the mare's ears and eyes, trickle down to her muzzle and gently caress the mare's lips, as soft as breath. Curls of light spread out along her neck and played in her silky mane – then there was another bright flash and the light whisked back inside the girl!

Jumana staggered against the doorpost. What had she just seen? Her eyes were playing tricks on her. They had to be, because this scene was impossible! And she was *still* seeing things because there was light in the stable, even though there was no lit lantern. Brightness was simply hanging in the air, illuminating everything, including the golden haired, amber-eyed girl who turned to look at her. The stranger's fingertips slid down the mare's nose as she gazed at Jumana. "Do not worry," she said. "I am not hurting her."

Jumana couldn't reply. A wave of dizziness had rendered her speechless and the next thing she knew, the intruder was at her side, leading her inside the stable and telling her to sit on some hay. Jumana followed her helplessly and sat when instructed. She didn't know what else to do.

"Just rest here. I will be finished soon," the strange girl said, and turned toward Hasna, the doctor's black mare. She flexed her fingers as she walked to the mare's head, and Jumana stared unblinking at the bizarre girl as she started the process all over again.

Hasna, do you know this human? Ah, she is Nefret and Aswan's girl. What else do you know of her? Is she kind? Is she trustworthy? Brave? Strong?

Latif, what do you think of her? Can she help us? She seems to be in shock. Is she too easily affected by unusual situations?

Rami, you wish to say something too?

Ah yes, I understand.

Thank you for your wisdom, my friends. We will ask for her help.

When the light flashed around Hasna, Jumana was on her feet – but this time, when the light whisked back inside the strange girl, the stable was instantly swamped in darkness. Swiftly, Jumana backed in the direction of the doorway. Would the girl attack her in the dark? She clutched for the lantern that most people kept at their stable entrance, thinking she could use it to protect herself, but her hand met only solid wall. In the darkness, she'd lost her sense of direction! Where was the doorway? Should she call for the doctor? Should she scream for help? Would anyone even hear her cries through the thick walls of the stable?

A small flame flickered and the girl was there, holding the newly lit lantern. Her eyes glowed like tawny embers in the light. "I am sorry for the darkness. I must reserve my strength and use artificial means of light now. So many are relying on me."

"Who… who are you? What are you doing here?" Jumana stammered. The wall was hard and cold against her back.

"I am Angelica, and there is no reason to be afraid. I am simply a servant to these, my beloved friends." She motioned to the horses standing behind her.

"A servant? What are you talking about?" Jumana glanced to her right. The door was only a few yards away.

"They need my help, so I help them."

"I… I don't know what you're talking about." Just a few steps and she could escape into the night, screaming for help.

"Come closer. I will show you." The golden girl held out her free hand.

Jumana shook her head and sidestepped toward the door. "I have to go. My horses, Nefret and Aswan –"

"Are heading away from the village, I know," said Angelica, finishing the sentence for her.

Jumana stopped short. "How did you know that?" she asked, her voice high and suspicious. Suddenly, she gasped. "You're the one who set them free! You're the thief!"

Angelica nodded. "Yes, I set them free," she admitted easily. "And I wish to tell you why, if you will let me. If you will accept what I have to say." Her eyes searched Jumana's as if she was trying to read the younger girl's mind.

"I won't. There are no good reasons to turn them loose. Don't you care that you might put them in danger?"

"I care very much. Will you listen to my explanation?"

Jumana edged farther along the wall to the doorway, slipped out the door, and paused. Angelica wasn't trying to stop her. Maybe she could afford to give the strange girl a minute to explain. "Okay," she said, turning back. "Tell me."

Angelica didn't hesitate. "I came here because Aswan and Nefret called me. They were frightened by terrifying visions that appeared in their minds, and as they reacted fearfully to these visions, they grew weak and ill."

Jumana could only stare into the golden eyes. What was this girl talking about? Was she insane? She shook her head. Angelica was right – she didn't believe her.

"Aswan and Nefret were only the first affected, but in time, the visions spread. I am attempting to help the horses by connecting to them, and hope to provide at least a partial shield for them, to guard them while I am gone."

"But that makes no sense." Jumana couldn't stop herself from speaking. "How can you..."

Angelica held up her hand. "Please hear the rest. You must understand. In short, it is up to me to journey to the malevolent power that is making them ill, and then discover how to combat it, so the horses can return to health and vitality. Aswan and Nefret have decided to help me in this mission. They have started on our journey, and soon I will join them."

"I think you're crazy." It was a whisper. "And I won't let you take Aswan and Nefret anywhere, especially across the desert."

"But we are not going alone."

"There's someone in this with you?" Jumana's voice was more accusing than questioning.

"I hope so. This spirit-shield I have given the horses is a terrible strain on me. I feel much like my friends here: confused and afraid. You alone are not affected by this unnatural horror and would be a great help to us. Will you come?"

"You're mad." Jumana didn't know what else to say. There was no other explanation for Angelica's unbelievable request. *Unless she's right!* The thought was completely unwelcome and Jumana tried to shove it through the back door of her mind.

But it *was* true the horses seemed anxious, wide-eyed, and even somewhat unaware. Her gaze shifted to Rami. His head was high and his shoulder muscles twitched. He stared off into a corner, a wild expression on his face. Latif's stance was packed with tension and Hasna was wet and trembling in a nervous sweat. None of the three were relaxed or sleepy, as Jumana would've expected in the middle of the night.

And now that she thought about it, her father had said Nefret and Aswan were acting strangely too. Nervous was the word he'd used.

"If you come closer, I can show you the pressure the horses feel," Angelica said, interrupting her thoughts. "Or if you prefer, Hasna can show you." When Jumana hesitated, Angelica continued. "Do not worry. You will only feel the fear second hand." Then she added in a soft, almost sad, voice, "If you think I am crazy, that I am deluded, then this is your chance to prove I am insane. If you feel nothing, you will know for certain that the words I have said here are false."

31

Reluctantly, Jumana nodded. She didn't trust this Angelica girl at all, but what she said made sense. This could be Jumana's opportunity to prove her words were mere ravings. "Okay, Hasna can show me. But I want you to go over there, to the back of the stable."

Angelica nodded, lowered the lamp to the bare floor, and stepped back. When she was standing against the far wall, Jumana walked to Hasna.

"Just put your hands on her forehead as you saw me do," Angelica instructed from across the stable.

Jumana appraised the girl again. Angelica was standing in a non-threatening pose and looked more tired than menacing. She didn't *seem* like she was going to do anything malicious. Jumana touched the mare's forehead lightly with all ten fingers.

"Now, close your eyes and breathe deeply."

Jumana wasn't about to close her eyes with the pale girl just a few yards away, so she narrowed them instead. She breathed deeply, allowing her lower chest and stomach to expand. The mare took a deep breath as well and her head sunk even closer to the floor.

"Now let her tell you how she feels."

Jumana took another deep breath. Nothing happened.

But of course nothing will happen. This is silly! Totally silly! And here I am, wasting time while Nefret and Aswan are wandering around loose. How stupid!

Suddenly, every reasonable thought was shoved from Jumana's mind. She could hardly remember who Nefret and Aswan were, let alone that they needed her to bring them home. A horrendous flood of terror pummeled every particle of her being, forced its way into her mind and twisted her thoughts, mutilated them. It was destroying her! She flung herself away from the mare and sprawled across the stable floor, her heart thudding like mad. The ghosts of terror wailed around her brain for a few more seconds, then finally faded away.

When she was fully aware of where she was again, Angelica was leaning over her with a concerned expression on her face. "Are you all right?" she asked, her voice the sweetest music after the horror.

The younger girl forced herself to a sitting position with trembling arms. "That's what Hasna is feeling?" Her voice was a croaky whisper. "That's what they're all feeling? And you too?"

Angelica nodded.

For the first time, Jumana met Angelica's extraordinary amber eyes without flinching, then she shifted her gaze to Hasna. The black mare stood quivering behind the girl. "Then I'll help you," she promised.

Abdullah drew Bastet to a trot when she stumbled the fourth time, thinking the ground must be too rough for safe travel now that the moon had set. But then she stumbled again, even at the slower pace. And again. What was wrong with his horse? He'd never known her to stumble once, let alone six times within a couple of minutes. In fact, she was known for her surefootedness and trustworthiness. She'd been acting strangely all night too, nervous and on edge, jumping at shadows. And her breathing was getting so loud, as if she couldn't get enough air into her lungs.

With a sudden lurch, Bastet fell to her knees, sending Abdullah up on her neck. His hand gripped her mane and he slid to the ground. The mare knelt in front of him until he pulled on her reins. Reluctantly, she rose to her hooves.

Abdullah pulled his matchbox from his pocket and, moving closer to Bastet, struck one of the matches. The tiny flame flared to illuminate the horse and draw the two pack camels from the darkness.

"What?" He couldn't stop his shocked exclamation. His reliable, steady Bastet was gone, and in her place stood a trembling, sweat covered creature with glazed eyes. He reached out to touch her shoulder and with a delayed reaction, she shied away, her movements stiff and jerky. Her breathing sounded more like roaring now.

"It's just me, Bastet," Abdullah murmured and stepped after

her. His voice seemed to soothe her and this time, when he reached out, she didn't move away. He touched her cheek and stared into her glassy eyes for a moment, stunned, and then the match went out.

"Hold steady, my friend," he whispered. "Let me see if I can find out what's wrong." He ran his hand along her neck to her shoulder and down her front leg. He thought the skin felt cool just above her hoof but he couldn't be sure. The coolness could simply be from the evaporating sweat running down her legs. But there was one more place he could check. Slowly, so he wouldn't startle her, he moved his hand along her neck toward her ears and touched the tip of one slack ear. It was positively frigid. Bastet was going into shock! But why?

Soothingly and carefully, he ran his hands over the rest of her quaking body feeling for injuries, but there wasn't a bump or cut anywhere. He even checked her hooves for stones, though he knew a stone in the hoof wouldn't make her ill, but still there was nothing.

So what was wrong with her?

Suddenly, Bastet groaned and lowered to the ground on shaking legs.

"Bastet!" He couldn't keep the alarm from his voice as he knelt beside her head and lit another match. The mare didn't respond to the sudden light and her horror-filled eyes stared off into space, unseeing.

"Bastet," he repeated, his voice full of despair. "What's happening to you? What's wrong?"

Abdullah looked in the direction of his largest camel, and though he couldn't see her in the darkness, he knew there would be room for him on the camel's back, despite her heavy load. Is that what he should do? Carry on and take his treasures to safety, then return with help for Bastet? He certainly didn't know what to do for her here, and there was a horse master in his village he could hire, now that he was rich.

But to leave her here, on the wild desert, unprotected! How could he bear to ride away from this horse he'd raised from a foal? And would Aisha ever forgive him if something happened to her Bastet? With the riches in the camels' packs, he could buy her ten horses, a hundred, even more – but Bastet was the horse she loved, the only one who was priceless to her. He couldn't leave the mare here alone. Could he?

Bastet decided his dilemma for him. With another groan, she stretched out flat on her side and her legs stiffened straight. Abdullah's heart sank. Bastet, his trustworthy mare and his daughter's beloved friend, was probably dying – and there was nothing he could do about it. Nothing, except rush back to the village where he and his family lived, hire the horse master, and bring him back to her. It was her only chance and he knew it. To stay by her side might give her comfort, if she was even aware of his presence anymore, but it wouldn't save her life.

His decision made, he lingered only long enough to pull the saddle from her back and whisper in the prone mare's ear, "I will return, Bastet. Be strong. Be strong for Aisha." Then he was on his feet, hurrying toward the largest pack camel.

He made the hissing sound that would signal the camel to kneel, and then settled in front of the pack the beast was already carrying. "Hut! Hut!" he yelled and the camel lurched to her feet and sprung into a trot. "Hut! Hut!" The camel broke into a lope.

Yet even at this speed, Abdullah knew it would take him all night, the next day, and most of the next night to get to his village and ride back with the horse master. He would probably be too late to save the mare. But because he loved her, because Aisha loved her, he would try.

Bastet, I am here. My dear one, do not be afraid. It is I.

I would have come sooner, my love, but your summons was so weak that I did not hear your call until the others were shielded and silent. I am so sorry. Please forgive me for not hearing you when you first thought my name.

My dear Bastet, let me help you now. Let me prove to you that I love you more than words can say. Please allow me to pull you back from the edge of this dark pit of the mind.

Moments after Angelica explained that another horse was summoning her and disappeared into the night, Jumana hurried from the doctor's stable. She wanted to catch up to Aswan and Nefret as quickly as possible. If they were feeling the horror that Hasna had shown her, she didn't want them to be alone. Even she kept picturing hideous monsters hidden in shadows and malicious forms creeping toward her through the night, and she had only experienced the terror second hand! Remembering Angelica's promise to join them soon was the only thing that seemed to keep her fear at bay. Though the strange girl had seemed terrifying to begin with, Jumana had changed her mind. At least Angelica was doing her best to help the horses.

Not like me, she thought and her mouth twisted ironically. *I fell backward, trying to get away from Hasna. I acted like a coward. But not Angelica. She moved toward the horses and is trying to shield them from the horror. As much as she can anyway.*

Jumana quickened her pace when she left the last building behind. Though the moon had set, stars lit her path enough that as long as she was careful she didn't stumble on the rough ground. If only Aswan and Nefret had taken the road to the south, then she'd be able to move much faster. She had to reach them soon, and then somehow, let them know they could rely on her in their confusion and fear. Maybe they'd even be able to draw strength from her presence.

She heard a clatter of rocks from ahead and stopped to listen. The desert was silent now, except for the rapid thud of her own heart, a sound that seemed to swell to fill the night. In her mind's eye, Jumana visualized dark, loathsome creatures slithering toward her, glaring at her with cruel eyes.

Don't be silly! There's nothing to be afraid of, she scolded herself. *The rattling sound has to be Aswan and Nefret. There's no one else out here on the desert.*

Yet, if it were the two horses, why were they still so close to the village? Were they really moving that slowly? Jumana peered ahead through the gloom, took a couple of steps, and saw movement. Relief crashed through her body when she recognized the dark forms ahead of her.

"Nefret! Aswan!" The mare stopped the second she heard Jumana call and turned her head to whinny. Aswan plodded another few steps, then stopped as well. Jumana rushed to Nefret's side and threw her arms around the mare's neck. She buried her face in the silky mane, then turned to Aswan and gave him his hug. The stallion nuzzled her back and whinnied weakly. Then slowly, purposefully, he pushed her aside and continued walking.

"Aswan?"

The stallion nickered again, but didn't stop and within a few steps, his iron gray coat blended into the night. Jumana turned to the mare. "He's right, Nefret," she said. Her fingers brushed lightly over the starred forehead. "We have to go, even if we don't want to. Even though we want to run the other way as fast as we can." She leaned forward to kiss Nefret on her nose. "So let's get started, beauty."

Bastet, my love, I do not understand. What you say does not make sense to me. Have I come too late to rescue you from delirium, or are you simply too disoriented to communicate what you really mean?

You say the darkness was taken from a hole in the earth, that it reached out with its wispy fingers and speared your mind? The darkness you speak of must be the evil that is consuming you. But how did it come from a hole in the earth? What was it doing there? And why is its touch so terrible? What has it done to you? Please help me understand.

You believe the end has come for all horse-kind? How? Why? I must comprehend if I am to know what to do, if I am to recognize how to save you.

One of your humans loosed the horror, and yet you say he is a good man. Again, I do not understand. How can a good man unleash such evil?

And now you say the darkness has split? What do you mean? I feel so frustrated at my ignorance. I do not comprehend what you are trying to tell me.

Bastet, even though we are connected now, I feel no answers to my questions. Your beautiful mind is half lost in shadow, my dear. Please, cling to your sanity. Be brave and hold on as long as you can. I must return to my companions now and continue our quest, if I am to save you. I will attempt to solve the mysteries you have given me along the way.

Please understand, Bastet, that is the only reason I would dream of leaving you now. But before I go, know this, I will come again, soon.

41

Sobekkare grimaced in her kingdom. The shield was now between her and all of the Enemies she'd discovered.

However, the situation wasn't as maddening as it might have been. She'd noticed a difference in the last shield when it was erected, a difference in strength. The protector had stretched itself too thin and was already weakening.

And still, Sobekkare was growing stronger, for some energy flowed past the failing shields, just like wind around a sail. In time, the shields would be worn to mere membranes, and then to nothing.

And then the protector would be at her mercy as well.

Jumana started jogging as soon as she was abreast of the two horses, and after a moment, Aswan and Nefret broke into a slow trot beside her. "Good boy. Good girl," she said in the most enthusiastic and encouraging voice she could muster, and lengthened her stride a bit more. She wanted to move them along a little quicker but at the same time, didn't want to go too fast. Angelica still needed to catch up and Jumana didn't want to push the horses too hard in their weakened state. They obviously were very affected by the mind numbing, energy depleting horror they were experiencing. They kicked up small stones as they trotted and occasionally one of them stumbled, yet still they kept to Jumana's pace.

A clear voice rang out behind her. "Jumana! Wait a moment!"

Both Aswan and Nefret stopped and Jumana turned to see the light from the stable lamp bob toward them. A tired smile touched Angelica's face when she greeted Jumana, then she turned to Aswan and placed her free hand on his satiny neck. A moment later, she moved on to Nefret and finally she turned to Jumana. "We must carry on quickly. Their suffering is deepening," she said, her voice tight with pain.

"They're getting worse?"

Angelica nodded. "Yes, too quickly. We must hurry."

"How do *you* feel?" asked Jumana.

"I am doing the best I can," the older girl stated, simply. She started to walk and Jumana and the horses fell in beside her.

"Can I help too? Maybe I can shield some of the visions too, if you show me how." Jumana swallowed. She couldn't imagine

43

anything worse than actually touching the horror again, but if it would help the horses…

"No," Angelica replied. "The best way for you to help them is to remain unaffected. We will need your clear thinking in this venture." She lengthened her stride further.

"Okay," said Jumana, trying to keep the relief from her voice. She broke into a jog, and Angelica ran beside her. After a few minutes of running in silence, Jumana spoke again, "Where are we going?"

"I am not familiar with this land, so I do not know where the terror is leading us," Angelica gasped. "However, we are going straight toward the evil's strongest point."

"We're running toward the mountains, to the wadis," said Jumana.

"What is a wadi?"

"A narrow canyon that goes back into the mountains. Most of them have tall cliffs on either side," Jumana panted as she ran. She was feeling a little breathless now too. "The people around here almost never go there. There's nothing in the wadis of any value." Suddenly, she gasped. "I just remembered something Father said last week. But it's probably nothing."

"Tell me anyway," prompted Angelica.

"He said a man came to the village to buy supplies. I wish I could remember his exact words. I think he said the man was camping in one of the wadis. Father assumed he was searching for treasure, like for a tomb or burial site or a mummy, so he could sell his findings to collectors in the city. But there aren't any tombs around here. No ancient king or queen would ever live way out here."

"The darkness was taken from a hole in the earth," breathed Angelica.

A shiver ran down Jumana's spine, despite the heat created by running. "Why do you say that?"

"It is an image one of the horses gave me. Bastet is her name.

She must have been the first affected, as she was in a very bad way when I came to her. I was able to help her only a little, she was so far gone. If only I had heard her earlier." Angelica blinked back rainbow tears. "Before I returned to you, Aswan, and Nefret, she tried to communicate a number of things to me, things she believed were important. One was that the darkness came from a hole in the earth, and would be the end of all horse-kind. Another was the fact that it was one of her humans who loosed the evil, though she said he is a good man. And she told me the darkness had split."

"What does all that mean?"

"The darkness is the malady, the terror-visions, I believe. But other than that, I do not understand *any* of the things she tried to tell me."

"It makes no sense. Didn't she say anything that we can use? Something a little clearer?" Jumana glanced over at Angelica as they jogged along. The older girl looked so tired and otherworldly in the lantern light, almost like an exhausted, wingless fairy. If only she had the powers of a fairy, or some other magical creature. But although Angelica appeared to be magical in some ways, clearly her power was limited. Was it enough to counter the dark force they were dealing with?

For a few minutes the only sound was hoof and foot on desert. Just when Jumana thought Angelica either hadn't heard her question or was lost in her own musings, the older girl spoke again. "It matters not how much I go over it. I have not heard of any thing like this before, and I have heard of many, many strange things."

"So if this Bastet was more advanced in the sickness than the others, how did she look when you saw her?" Jumana asked, wondering if maybe there was a clue in Bastet herself.

"She was failing physically, though she had no injury, and her mind was only halfway present, as if part of her consciousness was far, far away; somewhere I could not go," said Angelica, her voice pained. "I wish I could explain it to you better, but I cannot. Bastet is not the only one who speaks in riddles, I suppose. It is the terror-visions that make it so. They are beyond logical explanation in so many ways, and one has to use such vague and unreasonable terms."

Jumana swallowed nervously and for a second she slowed. More than anything, she didn't want what had happened to Bastet to happen to either Nefret or Aswan. "But she was breathing and her heart was pounding, right?" she asked.

"Her body was functioning, yes," Angelica clarified. "She seemed physically whole."

"So she'll be okay then," Jumana said hopefully. Angelica stopped and Jumana stopped beside her "Won't she?" she asked again.

"Jumana, I… I believe she is dying," Angelica finally said. "Or worse."

All the sorrow Jumana had ever heard was packed into those words, and in that instant she knew beyond a single doubt that Angelica would never harm her. She understood that the pale, ethereal girl intended no harm to anyone, for someone who could sound so broken-hearted and devastated at the fate of a horse she'd barely met could never wish ill on anyone, let alone do something that could harm them.

She reached out and touched Angelica's pale arm. "Don't worry. We'll save her. We'll save them all," she said, though she had no idea how. The only thing she knew for sure was that she, Nefret, Aswan, the horses of the village, and the unknown Bastet, were safer in Angelica's hands than they'd ever be anywhere else.

The shields were failing fast. She could feel them growing weaker, thinning out and becoming stretched. Whoever had placed them there had done so in vain. She, Queen Sobekkare, was far more powerful than the protector. She would win the minds of these Enemies. Soon she would possess them all, for the protector had been too ambitious, and tried to protect too many.

In fact, the shields were weakening so quickly that Sobekkare was starting to get a sense of the protector too now. And it wasn't human. Interesting. The protector wasn't an Enemy either, and it couldn't be a God, like Anubis or Horus. It was far too weak for that. The queen felt irritated; her experience was only telling her who the protector wasn't. It didn't say who it was.

However, since there seemed to be many Enemies in this era, it was possible there would be more Enemy protectors as well. She would be wise to investigate further. This time, she wouldn't underestimate her foes.

A long half hour later, they entered an obscure wadi, a narrow chasm carved into the mountains by natural forces centuries before. High inaccessible cliffs stretched to the sky on both sides and rocks of every size studded the wadi floor. The rough terrain forced them all to slow as the walls closed in. Jumana was incredibly grateful for Angelica's lantern. The wadi would be almost impassable without it. Huge chunks of the cliff had crashed down over eons of time and lay scattered, almost completely blocking their way in places. It was like an obstacle course, even with the light. They followed Angelica in single file, first Jumana, then Nefret, and finally Aswan, scrambling over rocks and around boulders.

When they reached a relatively clear area, Angelica bent over a burned out fire pit with sand kicked over it. "Someone was camping here only a short while ago," she said, her hand hovering over the pit. "The coals beneath are still hot."

Jumana looked around. "Maybe it was the man who came to our village. But why would he leave his campsite at night?"

"I do not know." The older girl straightened and held the lantern high, splashing light over the surrounding boulders and deep into crevices in the cliff.

"Look there," said Jumana and pointed. An edge of worn white cloth was showing from behind one of the rough boulders. Together they approached and Angelica's lantern revealed a canvas covered pile hidden behind the rock.

Jumana lifted a corner of the canvas to reveal a perfectly good

bedroll, some cooking pots, and additional camping gear. "Why would he leave so much stuff behind?" she wondered aloud.

"He may have had other stuff he would rather carry," Angelica suggested.

"Like what?" The second she asked it, Jumana knew. "This *has* to be the camp of the man who came to our village, and I bet he was looking for treasure, as Father guessed." She paused and looked at Angelica. "I think he found it. And there was so much to carry that he left most of his gear behind to fit more treasure onto his pack camels!"

"I think so too. And I believe he is also Bastet's man," Angelica added. "The evil is very strong here and Bastet communicated that her man was the one responsible for setting it free. He must have done so accidentally, when he found the treasure."

"Maybe it wasn't an accident."

"But he would not hurt Bastet on purpose, not if he is a good man, as she said."

"Some people don't care about horses," Jumana said, though she hated disagreeing with Angelica. "He might think it's more important for him to be rich than it is for Bastet to be well. She might be wrong about him."

"Yes, she might," Angelica whispered sadly, and sighed. She turned to look farther up the wadi, then back the way they'd come.

"So what do we do now?" Jumana asked, following her gaze.

"I cannot tell for certain where to go next. I have felt more confused since entering the wadi. The terror source is leading us still deeper inside these stone walls and yet there is a strong pull in the other direction as well, out onto the open desert again." She walked farther from the camp, her eyes searching the shadows for clues.

Jumana followed her. "So the terror has split, just like Bastet said," she said. "It's in the place where Bastet's man discovered the treasure, and yet some of it followed him too. Right?"

"I think so," Angelica said. She turned to face Jumana and the horses. "And now we need to decide our next step. Do we go to where the treasure was found, or do we follow Bastet's man?"

"Can't we do both?"

Angelica hesitated before replying. "I do not know how much longer I can last under this pressure, Jumana." Her voice was hushed, and Jumana detected a hint of embarrassment. "I am sorry. I do not wish to complain, but I am afraid that Aswan, Nefret, and I may not have the strength to pursue the second option, if our first choice is wrong."

"Don't apologize. It's not your fault. You're doing the best you can." Jumana bit her lip. Angelica did look very strained. Her face was paler than ever in the lamplight and seemed pinched. Her hair had even lost some of its luster. "I think we should follow Bastet's man," she said. "Even if part of the evil is still here, it can't do much more than it's already done, and we know the evil that went with Bastet was very strong. Otherwise, she wouldn't have gotten so sick, so quickly, right?"

"That seems wise," Angelica said thoughtfully. "But we must be sure or the consequences will be…" She shuddered. "…unspeakable."

"There is one more thing," Jumana added. "Bastet said the evil was loosed. Doesn't that mean it was *freed* from some sort of captivity? I don't really know how these things work, but isn't it possible there's no evil power left at all in the place Bastet's man found his treasures? Maybe it *seems* that way because it was there for so long it left a residue of its power behind, but really it's escaped."

Angelica looked impressed. "You are right," she said with a firmer tone. "I knew you would be a great help."

"So we should track Bastet's man, get the evil back from him, and then what? Return it to the tomb or cave or whatever it came from, and seal it back up?"

"That makes sense, and will be our plan for now. Let us get

51

started." Angelica's smile was tired when she held out the lantern. "Jumana, will you please lead the way?"

"Are you sure?" Jumana took the lantern reluctantly. She liked helping figure things out, but she didn't want to lead.

Angelica nodded wearily. Silence followed them as they retraced their steps down the wadi. When they finally stepped out onto the starlit desert again, Jumana turned around. "But Angelica, what do we do when we find the man? How do we convince the evil to follow us back? And then what about Nefret and Aswan? How will they bear being close to it while we're returning? Or you, for that matter."

The older girl looked at her with a dazed expression, then shook her head, blinked her eyes, and attempted to focus on Jumana. "I am sorry. What did you say?" Behind her, Nefret snorted and Jumana noticed that the mare looked almost as tired and confused as Angelica. Aswan rolled his eyes in fear as he stared back into the wadi.

Jumana didn't ask again. They really didn't have time for more long discussions. "I said 'don't worry'," she said. "We can do this. I know we can."

A ghost of a smile touched Angelica's eyes. "Thank you," she whispered.

Jumana smiled back and looked down at the ground. The tracks were easy to find. Yet still, before following the man's trail, she faced the open desert, closed her eyes, and took a deep breath. Could they do it? Was it even possible?

She flinched when Nefret touched her arm, then put her hand on the mare's neck. All the answers lay ahead of them, and there was nowhere to go but forward – so they had better get started.

Sobekkare paused. Here again was something new: one of the Enemies was different from the others. It was weaker, or physically weaker anyway. Yet it was stronger too, more resilient. Why?

For a moment, she raged around it, throwing every bit of terror at it that she could, until the creature writhed in horror on the floor. When a larger Enemy rushed forward, Sobekkare withdrew and watched them. The small Enemy climbed to its hooves as if it had hardly been touched and crowded up beside the larger one. It was trembling, yes. And frightened. But it wasn't terrorized. Why?

She was tempted to throw all her power at it again, to finish it off, but another movement from the larger Enemy drew her attention. The big one was stepping protectively in front of the small one.

Ah, that's its mother, she realized with a start. It's a young Enemy, a baby. Is that why it's so resistant, because it's still untouched by the sadness of the world?

There was only one thing she knew for certain: if she had ever had a child, she would've hated to see it die before she did. So in this one thing, she would be merciful. She would attack the young one after its mother had passed over. Until then, the baby Enemy would receive the same attention as all the others, but she wouldn't target it.

However, she would watch it, and maybe, even probe a bit. It would be nice to know for sure why it was quicker to recover than the full-grown Enemies.

As Jumana ran across the desert, she tried to take her thoughts in hand. She needed to stop worrying and start thinking, seriously thinking, so she could solve the problems before them. Right now, the obstacles seemed insurmountable, but there had to be a way around some of them at least. But how?

The first impossible task was how to catch up to a man riding a camel when they were on foot. Leaving his campsite at night, with hot coals still in his fire, implied that he was in a hurry to get to his destination. He was probably racing across the desert at the fast trot that camels were so good at, going more than twice the speed she was running.

Another problem was that Angelica and the horses kept lagging behind, too ill to travel as quickly as needed. Being close to the tomb had sapped their strength far too much, and following in the evil's path seemed to make them even worse. Jumana could see no solution to this problem either. Angelica, Aswan, and Nefret were going as fast as they possibly could. And even if they went faster, or if she left them behind, they would still be faced with the first problem: it was impossible for even her to match the camels' pace. With every second, Bastet's man was getting farther and farther away, and there was absolutely nothing she could do about it.

All I can do is my best, Jumana reminded herself. The thought gave her little comfort, but it did make her speed up. If her best was all she could do, then she'd better do it. She had to push herself as hard as she could every moment. One foot after the other, after the other, as quickly as possible. That was what she had to do. She just needed to hurry, hurry, hurry, faster and faster. On and on and on. Her feet pounded the sands, two strides to a second. The seconds turned to minutes, and the minutes dragged on, one behind the other. If she kept up this pace, she would make good time for someone on foot. Now if only Angelica and the horses could keep up. If only the camels would slow down.

And there were other problems too. Like, what was she going to do when she caught up to the man?

Suddenly her foot struck a stone. She lurched to the side and almost fell. The lantern flame flickered and Jumana quickly held it upright and watched, breathless, as the light nearly went out. She shut her eyes in relief when it flared up again. The last thing she needed was to have no light. It would be impossible to track the man and his camels then.

She looked back. Angelica and the horses were drawing near again. Good. She jogged on, careful to grip the lantern handle firmly. And the questions continued to present themselves. What were they actually chasing? Angelica called it a terror-vision, a sickness, but how was she supposed to manage something like that? Even if they caught up to the man, they couldn't put a terror-vision or a sickness into their pockets and carry it back. And if they somehow, someway, returned whatever it was to the wadi, how on earth were they going to find the tomb, or cave, or wherever the sickness had come from? She knew it must be well hidden, or it would've been discovered years ago.

But maybe I'm looking at it the wrong way, she considered. *Maybe instead of thinking of all these problems, I need to think of why the sickness is there at all.*

At that moment, more than anything, Jumana wanted to throw the lantern down and give up. Discovering the reason behind the sickness seemed the most impossible task of all! She blinked back tears as she stopped, leaned on her knees, and waited for Angelica and the horses to catch up. Gradually, her breathing slowed and her heart rate eased. Maybe Angelica would find it easier to concentrate now that they hadn't talked for a while. Maybe the strange girl had some answers for her.

But when Jumana's three companions stopped beside her, Angelica looked even worse, and so did Aswan and Nefret. The horses were wet with sweat and shivering, and Angelica's face seemed almost translucent she was so pale. Her eyes were a dull yellow and her hair the color of faded parchment.

"Do you want me to slow down?" Jumana asked the older girl. "Can I help in some way?"

Angelica shook her head. "Do not worry about us. We will do our best to keep up."

"Let's walk for a minute," Jumana suggested. She took Angelica's arm and when the older girl leaned on her, she was shocked at how light Angelica felt. "Can I ask you some questions, Angelica? Or are you too tired?"

"You may ask." Angelica's voice was barely audible.

"How do we carry this sickness or whatever it is, back to the tomb? How do we carry something that has no form?"

Angelica's breath came quick and shallow. "The sickness must be tied to a physical object or to a collection of objects. It has too much power to be solely in the spirit realm. It has to have…" Her voice faltered for a moment and Jumana waited. "It has to have at least one physical object as its base in order to exhibit such influence."

"At least one? So it could have the entire treasure as its base?" Jumana asked, incredulous. She knew there was no way they could talk anyone into letting a fortune go, not in this land of poverty and need. Not when, to Bastet's man, the riches would mean living easy for the rest of his life.

"It could…" Angelica stumbled and clutched Jumana's arm to save herself from falling. They stopped for a moment and Angelica composed herself before they continued to walk. "It could be tied to only one artifact in the treasure too. Try not to lose hope, Jumana. I *need* you to hope. You must not give up."

56

Jumana nodded. She was trying, but it was hard. "So how will we know which object is the right one?"

"I can tell when I touch it."

"And how will we get the man to give it to us? Even if it's just one artifact, it could be worth a lot of money."

"If he is a good man as Bastet said, and if he truly loves her, he will give it to us."

Jumana didn't respond. Angelica sounded so sure of this man, and she didn't want to add to their heap of problems by being negative. She *hoped* that the older girl was right, but couldn't help being doubtful. Money was hard to come by in her world, and riches nearly impossible. The man they were chasing might be a good man, even a very kind man, but would he give up a life of leisure and opulence for a horse?

Jumana didn't think so, but she said no more. If they didn't catch the man, there was no use in even worrying about it. Right now, it was time to run.

Bastet, can you hear me?

Bastet, are you there?

I feel a growing void within my heart. You are slipping beyond my reach.

Am I losing you forever, my friend?

Jumana's side was killing her and she was so tired. All she wanted to do was lie down and rest. Her leg muscles especially burned with fatigue. In most places, the sand was hard but, now and then, she hit soft sand and had to run through it until she was positive she couldn't take another step. Yet Angelica, Aswan, and Nefret still came behind her, slow but sure – and if they could do it, she could too.

She was focusing so much on taking the next step, and the next, and the next, that when she came to the dark lump in the sand, she almost fell on top of it. She stopped just short of the prone mass, and the lantern light jumping and dancing in her shaking hand made patterns of light and dark flow over the horse's side. It could only be Bastet.

"Angelica! Hurry!" she yelled and placed the lantern carefully in the sand. She bent over Bastet's head. "How are you, Bastet? You're such a brave girl. Angelica told me all about you. Now you hold on. She'll be here any second, okay?" The mare didn't even quiver an ear and her eyes remained shut. Was she dead?

Heavy breathing came up behind Jumana, and she looked back – and leapt to her feet in shock! Angelica was hardly recognizable. Her hair was completely white now, and she looked so weak and gaunt that Jumana could feel only pity for her. Aswan and Nefret didn't look much better and stood with their heads to their knees. Their breath came in roaring gasps, and there was no longer any expression of fear in their eyes. They were too exhausted to be frightened of anything, too fatigued to care.

Jumana stood back as the older girl knelt, graceful despite her emaciated appearance. Pale fingers lightly brushed the mare's cheek and Bastet's large dark eyes quivered.

"She's still alive," Jumana whispered, relief washing through her.

"In a fashion, yes," said Angelica, her voice a murmur. "Though she is not aware of us, her heart still beats. She still draws breath."

"Is there anything we can do?"

"There is." Angelica looked up and met Jumana's gaze. "There is only one thing we can do, Jumana. But I am afraid you will not like it."

Sobekkare smiled on her throne. The first Enemy she'd attacked had just begun its slide into her kingdom, and two more were close to following. Only the protector was stopping their full descent, and the protector was almost useless now. Soon the shields would be worn to nothing, and Sobekkare could claim the Enemies she'd attacked this night.

Not that she wanted to bring all the Enemies to her kingdom. Tomorrow's victims would be allowed to die. She only wanted a few. She was bored with her amusements and mock battles, and a few Enemies for her soldiers to fight would be wonderful. A few to play her war games with would be lovely.

And besides, she was curious about these creatures. Handled carefully and controlled properly, their presence might turn out to be enjoyable. She smiled again. Enjoyable for her, that is. Not for them.

And if they didn't cooperate and play her war games? Well, she'd just banish them to the dark sands. She'd send them off to wander forever, alone with nothing but the gray, stretching into eternity.

It was just payment for what they'd done to her.

"Why won't I like it? What do you want me to do?" Jumana asked, her voice wary. "You can't ask me to leave you," she added, suddenly realizing what Angelica might say. "I can't go on alone and just leave you here to… to…" She stopped. She didn't want to say the word.

"You will not be alone," Angelica replied. "Nefret shall go with you."

Jumana looked up at her beloved mare, swaying back and forth on weak legs behind Angelica. "Nefret? But she's not strong enough."

"She will be. And you shall ride her. That should allow you to catch the man and his camels, and enable you to return the sickness to its source."

"But how can she? I don't understand." Jumana moved to Nefret's side and stroked her wet neck. "She's not going to suddenly feel better, unless…" She gasped. "No!"

"Yes, I will withdraw the remains of my power from the other horses and give everything to Nefret," said Angelica feebly, confirming Jumana's theory.

"But what about the others? How will they survive?"

Angelica grimaced in pain. "Jumana, you must realize there is no other way," she whispered. "Our only assets are my energy, Nefret's speed, and your ability. We must use both to our best advantage. You and Nefret must pursue this man and save the horses. The way things are now, we will never catch him, and then my energy will be gone, and it will be too late for us. Surely you must see that?"

"But what if I can't do it? What if the horses die?" Jumana's voice was desperate. Angelica couldn't leave her alone with this weighty responsibility. "What if *you* die?"

"There is no other way."

"But Angelica, I need you to help me," she pleaded frantically. "Even if I catch up to him, he won't listen to me. He won't give me the artifacts we need. Can't you give Nefret strength and still keep enough to come with us?"

"There is not enough left to keep us both well." Angelica paused and took a deep breath. "I believe you can do this, Jumana. I have faith in you. You know what must be done, and how to do it. You *will* catch up to this man and his camels, ask him for the artifact or artifacts that spread this sickness, and return to the tomb as quickly as you can, because you *must*. That is the only way we will be saved."

"But…" Jumana turned to bury her face in Nefret's mane. Angelica trusted her to save them, but all Jumana could see was the dreadful impossibility of the task before her. There was no way she could do what Angelica expected of her.

Yet she had no choice but to try. Angelica was right. They had only one chance to catch up to Bastet's man – by Angelica giving all her light-energy to Nefret.

So that's what they would do. And she would try her best.

And she would fail, of that she was sure.

Hasna, be brave. I must withdraw my strength from you. Please forgive me.

Goodbye, Latif and Rami. Please know that I would not leave you if I had a choice, any choice.

Amala and Maysa, we are doing our best to save you. Do not despair. I know it is especially hard for you, Maysa dear, for you will now watch your foal fall into darkness. How I wish I could avert this horror for you all!

Ali, Shadi, Kalila, and Zara, fare well, my loves. I know it seems I am abandoning you all. I am so sorry. Please believe that I do not want to do this. Please believe that this is our only hope.

And Aswan, the first connected to, and the last from which I will withdraw, will you forgive me? I would give anything, everything, to save you, but I have nothing more to give. Please do not blame me too much.

Goodbye, my loves.

In one instant, everything shifted. The shields were gone from all the Enemies but one. Sobekkare couldn't contain her pleasure, her fulfilment, her joy! In a matter of minutes, the Enemies would be weak enough to start pulling into her realm.

She could sense the protector quite clearly too, now that its shields had fallen, and she still didn't recognize what it was. Though it was similar to the Enemies in its heart, it certainly wasn't one of them. In fact, in form, it looked like a human girl – and yet it obviously wasn't human either.

Should she bring it to her kingdom as well? She was curious about the creature, that was for certain. And she might learn something about it through interrogation, though she wouldn't get her hopes too high. It probably wasn't very smart – it was a servant of the Enemies, after all. But if she asked it only simple questions, she might learn something of value.

Jumana heard a groan come from behind her and spun around.

"No!" she shrieked as Aswan sunk to the ground beside Nefret. "Aswan!" She dropped to the ground in front of him and held his head between her hands. For a split second, the stallion focused on her, then his eyes rolled back and he groaned again. With labored breath, he pulled away from her to stretch out flat on his side.

"Aswan?" Jumana said in a whisper. Tears were running down her cheeks. "Aswan?" she managed to choke out once more, but the gray didn't respond. She stroked his cheek and fought to control her sobs. If she was going to save him, she couldn't dissolve into an emotional puddle. She had to act.

"We have to save him, Nefret," Jumana said and staggered to her feet. "We have to get that whatever-it-is back inside that tomb."

Nefret looked different – much more vivacious, much more like the Nefret Jumana had known her entire life. The mare's ears were forward and she was peering at Aswan with concerned, aware eyes.

Angelica's done her magic, Jumana realized. *Nefret has her energy. Poor Aswan, and Bastet, and the others.*

Poor Angelica! The thought sliced through Jumana's mind and she hurried to the girl's side. Angelica lay still beside Bastet. Her dry, brittle hair fanned around her head like cracks in ice and her face was stone white in the lantern light.

"Angelica, are you all right?" Jumana asked, then pinched her lips shut. Of course Angelica wasn't all right. What a stupid thing to ask! She touched the girl's shoulder. "Angelica, keep some energy for yourself. Even just a little."

Angelica's eyes opened and she feebly shook her head. "You must go, Jumana." Her whisper was almost inaudible. "You must save us."

Jumana nodded, filled with too much emotion to form words. She clambered to her feet.

"Remember, I…" Angelica's colorless lips stilled and she shut her eyes.

The younger girl bent closer. "I'm listening, Angelica. Remember what?" What words of wisdom did the older girl have to offer? What clues to help Jumana accomplish her task? Two tears fell from Jumana's eyes and plopped onto Angelica's arm.

Angelica opened her eyes. "Remember," she repeated with great effort. "I believe in you."

My energy is gone. I am being sucked into terror. It is closing around me, a suffocating vice. Darkness. All is darkness.

I have never felt so alone! Where are my beloved ones? Bastet are you here? Aswan, can you hear me?

Nothing. I hear nothing. Not a whisper. Not a sigh. Only perfect stillness. It is as if I am at the heart of death.

Yet I am not dead. What is this dark realm? Where am I? I am lying on gritty ground – sand – it must be. And I am solid here. My entire being, including my body, has slipped inside this realm.

Why am I here? Who has brought me to this sinister place?

Using her legs and a single-handed grip on Nefret's mane, Jumana guided the mare across the desert. More tears rolled down her cheeks as they cantered along. Leaving Angelica, Aswan, and Bastet behind was the hardest thing she'd ever done.

She leaned forward and encouraged Nefret to run faster. They had to catch up to the man as quickly as possible. Nefret answered the request with a renewed burst of speed and her long mane whipped out to touch the lantern glass. Jumana smelled a whiff of burning hair and almost lost her seat as she jerked the lantern even farther to the side. Frantically, her eyes scanned Nefret's red mane. Thank goodness, there was no flame.

And thanks to Nefret for being so smooth gaited! Otherwise, Jumana didn't know how she'd stay on the mare's back. Racing over the desert, with no saddle or bridle, one hand clasping mane and the other holding the lantern as far from the horse as she could, was no easy task. Jumana glanced down at the ground whipping past. They were still on target. She could see the camels' tracks in the sand. It was odd how Nefret hadn't wavered from the trail even once. Could the beautiful horse know they were following the tracks?

"You do, don't you?" Jumana whispered and wished she had a third hand so she could pat the mare's neck. "You're the smartest horse in the world, Nefret."

They topped another sand hill and Jumana raised her eyes to the horizon. The desert stretched wide in every direction and for a moment, she was overwhelmed again with the immensity of her task. As Nefret galloped down the decline, her thoughts turned again to the myriad unanswered questions. Would she catch him in time? And then get him to give her the right artifact? Or artifacts?

An abrupt coldness swept around her heart. She'd just thought of something else. Something terrible. How was she to know which was the right artifact? Angelica was the one who'd said she'd recognize the right item when she saw it, not Jumana. So even if the man said she could take the object or objects, she wouldn't know which one to take!

"What am I going to do?" she said in despair and Nefret laid one ear back to listen. "How will I know which is the right one? Or if there's more than one? Or if *any* of them are right?"

But Nefret had no answers. She just ran on and on, into the night.

Now that my being has adjusted to the lack of light, I can sense a little in this strange place. Dark sands stretch around me, bleak and unwelcoming. Midnight air above and around. No stars. There is nothing else. No living thing. No sigh. No breath. Not even grass, nor wind. What a terrible place to be captive. It is a dead land.

And yet, I live on. In fact, I have more energy here than I did above, enough to walk and move about. Could less energy be needed to function in this strange world? Or do I simply have more because I am isolated from the horses that need me above? I am no longer in connection with Nefret. I pray that the energy I gave her will be enough for her to accomplish her task.

Wait, what is that? A darkness approaches in the eternal night. And now I hear a sound. Someone is coming!

Jumana was concentrating so much on keeping her seat and looking for tracks that she didn't notice Nefret was failing until the mare slowed from a gallop to a canter. With the slower gait, she felt she could loosen her grip on the mare's mane and she reached down to touch Nefret's shoulder. The horse was covered with sweat again. And she felt chilled.

There was only one explanation. The energy that Angelica had given Nefret was fading. They were running out of time already.

But it was too soon. Far, far too soon!

A being is coming closer to me. I cannot see what it is yet but I will face it bravely. I will show it I am not afraid of the type of creature that calls this place home!

Oh Bastet! It is you, my lovely Bastet! How relieved I am to see you! How overjoyed that we have found one another in this horrid place!

At the very least now, we are not alone.

They were falling, one by one, into her kingdom. Sobekkare could feel their fear, taste their terror, and she reveled in it. Even the strange protector was afraid, or she knew it must be. How could it not in this dark place where the ancient queen ruled supreme?

And what lay before the Enemies and their useless protector now? Sobekkare smiled. An eternity of her revenge!

She needed to prepare her army for the Enemies' arrival. But first, she would ensure the creatures were too exhausted to fight effectively against her soldiers. The Enemies had ripped through her armies in the other world, and the last thing she desired was for them to do the same here. That would be far too humiliating!

When Nefret tried to slow to a trot, Jumana pushed her harder. In her opinion, trotting took as much energy as cantering, and yet didn't cover as much ground. Nefret struggled onward as Jumana kept up a melody of encouraging words, and for a while at least, her words seemed to hold Nefret's fears at bay. The mare held her ears back, listening, and cantered on and on, blowing heavily in time to her strides. Up one sand hill and down another. Around that large outcropping, and then through a soft dune. Up another hill. Slide down. On and on and on she went.

Suddenly she stumbled and went down on her knees, sending her rider flying forward. Jumana hit the sand hard, curled into a ball, and lay still, wanting more than anything to never move again. She heard Nefret climb to her hooves, shy at some imaginary monster, and stop again a few yards away. And wait.

But Jumana couldn't seem to make herself stand up. She didn't even want to turn her head to look at the mare, let alone continue their hopeless mission. There was no point. She wasn't going to succeed, and it would be her fault when the horses and Angelica died. She was a failure, a miserable, laughable failure. Tears blurred the cold stars above her, turning them to smears in the night sky.

Almost the worst thing though, was that she hadn't failed *yet*. She still had to go through the motions: try and try and try and still not catch up to the man. Or if she somehow managed that, then either not be able to convince him to give her the artifact or pick out the wrong one. She still had to go through all the pain and heartache and sadness of *failing*, knowing countless others would die when she did. If only she could just walk away. If only she could just go home and forget this entire nightmare had ever happened.

But she couldn't. If she turned around and went home, she'd have to live with the guilty knowledge that she'd betrayed Aswan, Nefret, Angelica, and the others, for the rest of her life. If she didn't do *everything* she could to save them, she would be haunted until her dying day. There was no doubt in her mind that it would be an unbearable thing if they died, but it wasn't as completely intolerable as both having them die *and* her abandoning them to their fate.

She had to keep trying, even if it was hopeless.

It wasn't until she sat up that she realized how dark it was. "Nefret?" The mare nickered to her, and Jumana climbed to her feet and looked about. There was Nefret, a dark hulk in the night. And something at her feet, something glimmering in the starlight. The lantern. Extinguished!

Jumana wanted to sag down on the desert again. She wanted to beat the ground with her fists and scream out her frustration! How was she to track the man now? Even if she somehow got Nefret to continue on fast enough to catch him, how was she going to find him if she couldn't follow his tracks? It was hopeless! Hopeless!

But she didn't allow her knees to buckle. She didn't fall to the desert. She'd already faced her hopelessness and knew she had to keep going, no matter what. Resolutely, she walked to Nefret and stroked her neck, then scrambled onto her back. The mare would have to track the man. Both her ears and eyes were superior to human senses, even with Nefret being impaired by the sickness. Jumana would trust her to continue on the camels' trail.

"Let's go, beauty," she murmured, her hand lingering over the cold, sweaty neck. "Just one step at a time. That's all we can do. One step at a time."

Aswan. You have come to us as well. Yes, it truly is Bastet and myself. Have no fear.

It seems as if we are all to be sent to this place. As the others are overcome, I believe they will join us here too. What a tremendous relief! We shall be together again.

Let us wait for all to arrive, then we will find out where 'here' is. Hopefully we can discover what, or who, has brought us to this place. And why.

Nefret only trotted now, and not even an extended trot at that. Though Jumana pushed her as hard as she could bear, the mare couldn't seem to go any faster. Soon Jumana planned to slide from her back and run at her side, but for now the horse was still moving faster than the girl could run. She tried not to think of how strong Nefret used to be as they trotted along. Arabians were known to be wonderful endurance horses, and Nefret was one of the best. Normally, she could canter all day across the desert and still have enough energy to race the last mile toward home. Knowing the proud horse that Nefret was, Jumana found it heartbreaking to watch the mare fade before her eyes.

Suddenly Nefret stopped, and for a moment her head was high, her ears pricked forward. Then her fatigue brought her head low again. Her ears sagged sideways.

Jumana focused ahead. Was she seeing things, or were there really tiny pinpricks of flickering lights in front of her? What could they be? Some type of glowing insect? Or something farther away? She reached out with her hand, but felt only air. They must be farther away then.

She slid from Nefret's back. "What are they, beauty?" she asked, her hand on the mare's cool cheek. "Can you tell? They look like campfires, but why would anyone be camped in the middle of nowhere?"

The mare didn't respond in any way and, disheartened, Jumana gently took the long forelock in hand to lead her forward. Nefret followed sluggishly.

79

Jumana crept toward the lights as quietly as she could. She was relieved that Nefret's lethargy made her hoofbeats barely audible and her breathing wasn't too loud yet. The mare's exhaustion would probably stop her from whinnying to any other horses too, so they should be able to approach the lights unnoticed.

Jumana's heart fluttered nervously within her chest as she came closer. She'd never been this far from her village in this direction before, and her home – her safe place – seemed too far away. If only she knew the lay of the land. The lights in front of her could be those of another village for all she knew, though with only three lights it would have to be very small. Or it could be the camp of a nomadic tribe, which might mean posted guards. Or the lights could mean a common stopping place, like an oasis, where small groups of travelers camped overnight. This thought was the most intimidating of all. Thieves and murderers might be nearby if there were small caravans to rob. What if she came across the camp of some bandits? She had to be extremely careful.

But if it's an oasis, Bastet's man might be there too, she thought, trying to look on the bright side. *Maybe he stopped for the night and is sleeping beside one of the campfires right now*. For the first time in hours, she felt a small twinge of hope.

By the time they reached the first tree, Jumana could see that the lights were indeed from campfires. Three campsites were spaced evenly around a pool, and a dozen palm trees were illuminated in each fire's warm glow. There was water here, and therefore, vegetation. The fires danced in the darkness and flickered against the straight trunks, their flames brave in the moonless night.

"You stay here, Nefret," Jumana whispered. The mare sighed and the girl cringed. Even Nefret's sigh was loud in the stillness. If Bastet's man heard, he'd be forewarned of her presence. And even if he was the good person that Bastet believed, there were at least two additional campsites at the oasis. Jumana certainly didn't want to find out the hard way what kind of people were staying there.

"I'll be back soon, beauty," she murmured, stroked Nefret's quivering neck one last time, then moved toward the nearest light. She would have to *become* stealth.

Maysa, there she is: your foal, Amala. She has stepped from the darkness, the last to arrive of the village horses. Let us go meet her. She appears confused and very frightened, the poor thing. She will be comforted when she realizes we wait for her.

My little Amala, come to us. It is so good to see you, my dear. Finally, we are reunited.

And now, all, please gather round. I wish to discuss our next course of action with you.

But wait! What is that? Do you hear? A trumpet sounds! And again.

Are we are being summoned?

My loves, do we answer the trumpet's call? I believe we should, but the choice is yours. I will respect your wishes.

Jumana felt even more defenseless after she left Nefret. The mare, though weak, could still warn Jumana of someone's approach or of someone hiding in the darkness waiting to spring out at her.

But I can't put her in danger, Jumana reasoned. *And it's better if she has a rest anyway. She's so tired, and we still need to travel all the way back to the tomb. If I can get the artifact, that is.*

She stopped to listen. Maybe Nefret couldn't listen for danger for her, but she could try to sense it herself, if not half so expertly. She wasn't completely helpless.

Someone inhaled to her left, and then exhaled, long rhythmic breaths that meant sleep. Jumana froze and tried to penetrate the darkness with her eyes. There at the foot of that bent palm tree, that's where the sound was coming from. Someone must be leaning against the trunk, and sleeping. But why would they be away from the campfire?

A guard, she realized suddenly. *That's who it is! And he'll probably have a weapon!*

Holding her breath, she silently backed the way she'd come. The soft snores faded to nothing. When she felt she'd retreated far enough, Jumana stopped to catch her breath. That was too close for comfort! She'd come back later and check this campsite from the other side.

She moved swiftly toward the second campsite. An elaborate tent was situated close to the campfire – a tent that looked big enough to house an entire family and a few horses. Many nomadic families kept their fine horses inside their tents at night to keep them safe from thieves.

Though Jumana couldn't see anyone, she knew the camp didn't belong to Bastet's man. The tent was far too big for a man traveling alone. Also, he'd left the wadi only a few hours before. He wouldn't have had time to both travel to the oasis and erect a tent like this. And then there were the dark lumps dotting the sand on the far side of the tent. Were they a small herd of resting camels? She moved a bit closer. Yes, that's exactly what they were. This definitely wasn't the right camp, and there was no point in risking further investigation.

Jumana hurried on, and a few minutes later was peering around a bush at the third campsite. This one was much smaller and therefore much more likely to belong to Bastet's man. There was no tent and only one person huddled inside the bedroll beside the campfire. It could easily be him!

Jumana dropped to the ground and wriggled closer. She wanted to get close enough to see if there were any artifacts in the small pack lying at the man's head. There was no point in waking him to ask for the object if he was the wrong man.

She was in the fire's glow now. Closer, closer, she squirmed. She could see part of his face, shining in the firelight. She swallowed nervously. He didn't look like a kind person. In fact, he looked hard and callous, even in sleep. His face was permanently etched in frown lines.

But I shouldn't judge him too quickly, Jumana reminded herself. *My grandfather has a furrowed face too, and he's the nicest man in the world*. She leaned forward, hoping to see more detail in the man's bearded face. His mouth fell open and a rumbling snore poured out. Then his eyelids fluttered.

Fear lanced through Jumana's heart and she flattened herself to the ground. She listened, dreading to hear his exclamation of surprise and then his shout, but there was only the subtle rustle of cloth as he adjusted his position. Then, the snoring continued.

Slowly, she counted to ten and looked up. The man was still asleep, his face pointing to the sky. A flash of firelight on metal caught her eye, and Jumana gasped aloud. A rifle! The man was sleeping with his rifle for protection. It had been hidden by his blankets before, but now it lay in plain sight, a few inches from his left hand. She wouldn't dare go for the artifact now, even if it were in the small pack.

She peered past the man and into the shadows, and a subtle movement caught her eye. A creature was tethered to a tree behind the man. She could barely perceive its presence in the night, but it had to be one of the camels – and the camels would have the larger packs with them. She should've checked the animals first!

As quickly and quietly as she could, Jumana slithered back the way she'd come. When she was hidden in the darkness once again, she rose to her feet to circle toward the movement. She watched the man as she skirted the edge of the firelight. He was still sound asleep, lying on his back and snoring, with the gun close at hand.

She turned her attention to the darkness ahead of her. There, another movement. She honed in on the shadow beneath the tree, and stepped closer.

But the form in front of her was too small to be a camel. It had to be a horse. Jumana's heart plummeted as she crept nearer. The horse's silhouette was faint in the shadows, but she recognized an elegant neck, a strong back, a fine head – and splayed legs and lopping ears: a stance all too familiar to her now. This horse was ill. The sickness was spreading!

You poor thing, she thought and reached out. The horse's eyes glistened with fear and she withdrew her hand. She was only frightening it further. She sighed quietly. Yet another life on her shoulders, another afflicted creature that would either live or die depending on whether she succeeded or failed in her mission.

"I will do my best for you, my friend," Jumana whispered, then she turned and hurried silently back the way she'd come. There was nothing she could do for the horse here. Just like with the others, the only way she could help was to return the artifact to where it belonged. Now if only it was at the first campsite, the one with the sleeping guard.

"Oh no." Jumana's whisper was full of dismay. She hadn't been thinking clearly at all! The first campsite couldn't belong to Bastet's man either. A man traveling alone wouldn't light a fire and then fade off into the trees to guard it. Instead, he'd curl up near the fire to keep warm just like the man at the last camp, with his camels tethered nearby. The first campsite had to belong to a group of people with one guarding while the others slept.

Jumana shivered and picked up her pace. The night was becoming colder. It must be more than half gone by now, and she'd just wasted a tremendous amount of precious time checking the campsites.

But what was she to do next? If the guarded campsite didn't belong to Bastet's man, then where was he? There were so many possibilities. He could be camping at the oasis without a campfire. Or camped somewhere else. Or worst yet, he could still be racing across the desert, getting farther away from her every second!

Nefret can track him, she remembered as she hurried along. *I'll have to let her lead me to the man, even if it means letting her go into danger.*

She stopped short and looked about. This seemed the right place, the place she'd left Nefret. So where was the mare? Had she wandered off? Jumana turned a full circle. Maybe she'd come to the wrong place. But there was the guard's bent tree silhouetted in the distance, just where it should be. And here, a roughness to the sand, as if it had recently been marked by hooves. It had to be the right place.

Maybe she went for a drink, Jumana thought fearfully. *Or maybe she's lying down somewhere, hidden by the night and too sick to stand.*

"Nefret?" The whisper seemed loud and Jumana waited breath-lessly. "Nefret," she repeated when there was no response. "Are you there?" Only silence.

"Hey!" A distant shout. "Wake up! Look what I found!"

Jumana clutched her hands to her chest. That yell could only mean one thing! Nefret had been captured! For a moment, she felt paralyzed. What was she to do? Why was yet another thing going horribly wrong?

Bending low, she ran toward the voice. She avoided the guard's tree as she sped along, even though in the back of her mind she knew there was probably no point. The guard had to be the one who'd found Nefret.

She stopped behind the last tree before the flickering campfire and peered around the spindly trunk. She could tell with a single glance that the campsite didn't belong to Bastet's man. She'd been right in her reasoning. There were three men at the fire, not one, and they all stood around the sagging mare.

Jumana forced back a shocked gasp now that she could see Nefret clearly in the firelight. She looked beyond terrible, far too sick to care that she'd been captured. Their race across the desert had cost her dearly! And how was Jumana going to get her away from her captors, when Nefret hardly had the strength to stand?

The trumpet still sounds in the distance, just as far away as when we first heard it. All around splay dark sands. There are no features, no landmarks – just barren sand forever.

We are all tired. Though we do not need as much energy in this land, we are near exhaustion. Is this the design of whoever brought us here: to weaken us before we reach them? To make us too tired to defend ourselves?

We must continue on as long as we can, my dears. Come to me, Amala. Will you walk at my side? You, who are the smallest, can show through your example, the strength and fortitude we all need. You can be the inspiration to all those who follow.

And, my companions, we may be wise to pretend we are more tired than we are, and keep some strength in reserve. If this is a plan to drain us of our energy, we may want to arrive at the trumpet's call not quite as exhausted as our captor expects.

Jumana's knees felt weak as she pulled back behind the tree and leaned against the trunk. After all their efforts, all their sacrifices, was this how it was going to end? With the other horses and Angelica lost forever, and Nefret in the clutches of strangers? With the man they were pursuing carrying merrily on his way, unwittingly spreading destruction and death to all the horses around him? And with Jumana completely helpless to do anything about it? If only something would go right for a change, then she might have a chance to avert the doom that hung over so many innocent beings.

Grasping at her courage, she peered from behind the tree again. The men's voices were so low she could only catch a word now and then, but she guessed they were talking about Nefret. Maybe they were wondering if she belonged to another of the travelers at the oasis, or if she was a stray. Or they might think her presence meant there was a thief about, a thief who had left his horse be-hind while creeping forward to steal from the camps.

"No! She's too fine to turn loose." The men's voices were getting louder.

"But look at her. There's something wrong with her." The man dressed in brown gestured to the mare. "She's sick."

"But if she recovers, we can get a lot of money for her." The first man said, even more stridently. "Look at that head and long neck, the strong back. Maybe she's not sick at all. Maybe she's just frightened." He sounded frustrated, irritated.

The brown-robed man rubbed his beard and turned to their

companion, the one who hadn't spoken yet. He said something too low to hear and Jumana guessed he was asking the third man's opinion.

The third man waited a moment before responding. He looked at Nefret, at her sweaty shoulders shimmering in the firelight, at her trembling legs, and then to each of the men in turn. Finally he spoke, and his voice reached Jumana easily, not because he was yelling, but because his voice was rich and deep. "She's a fine mare. We take her," he said and Jumana's heart sank. "But we have to leave now, before her owner shows up."

The first man nodded immediately and knelt to collect his bedroll. The man in brown – the guard, Jumana guessed – looked down at his neat blankets. The forbidden sleep he'd had while standing guard obviously hadn't been enough. No doubt he was regretting his impulse to bring Nefret to the attention of his traveling companions.

Please, please, say something more. Ask if you can have some time to sleep first. Say again that she's sick. It's so obvious that she's not well!

But the brown-robed man looked up at their leader and nodded agreement.

"Put her with the others while we pack up," the leader instructed.

The tired guard sighed, picked up a rope from beside the fire and tied it around Nefret's neck, then with a tug, led her past the campfire and into the shadows.

The Enemies were hardly moving anymore. Sobekkare could sense their pace as she sensed all things in her kingdom, as if all that happened were a part of her. The strength of these Enemies was gone. Sobekkare was thrilled! She had waited far too long for this repayment. At last, the fruiting of her vengeance!

Her soldiers too were becoming impatient. They wanted their revenge on these creatures as well, though not a fraction as much as their queen did, to be sure. Sobekkare called out to them in her mind, telling her brave battle-worn to ready themselves. Then she turned her mind back to the Enemies and their protector. She would transport them just beyond the range of her soldiers' vision. She could already imagine the roar that would burst from her army's throats when they saw the Enemies – the bloodlust roar. It had been too long since she'd heard it.

When the transport was complete, she speared each soldiers' mind with a last warning. They were not to seriously maim the Enemies or the protector. That was their only limitation. That was the only thing she asked of them.

Then she settled back into her throne and watched the army mill about below her. Any second now, any second, the Enemies would come into view.

What fun!

Jumana quietly skirted around the campfire light as the men packed their gear. They were moving swiftly and she knew she only had minutes until they were ready to go. She had to get Nefret away before they started preparing their animals for the journey.

A snort burst from the darkness before her and she stopped short. More horses. These men weren't riding camels either. Were their horses sick as well? If so, she might find an opportunity in their fear. The sickness made them afraid, even of familiar things, and they would probably run from their masters – which could give her and Nefret the precious moments they needed to escape.

Slowly, she edged toward the sound of stamping hooves. There they were: four horses spaced evenly along a rope stretched between two trees, with the horse on the end being Nefret.

"Hold steady," she breathed as she approached the first horse with her hand out. The animal raised its head in alarm. "Hold steady," she repeated, even quieter. "I won't hurt you, I promise."

The horse jerked back against its rope. It wasn't about to let Jumana remove the headstall. But she could still untie it. Working quickly, she untied the knot, and then keeping the lead rope in one hand, moved on to the next horse. Within seconds, this horse too was untied, and Jumana pulled the two toward the third horse.

Unfortunately, the third horse didn't like the others so close to it. It threw its weight back against its tether and kicked out at the other two with both back hooves. The untied horses sprung away as one, jerking their ropes from Jumana's hand, and trotted away

with stiff movements. The third horse watched them go, wild eyed and agitated. Jumana glanced back at the fire. The men hadn't noticed yet.

"Hold still, buddy," Jumana whispered desperately. Her fingers tugged at the tightened knot and, finally, the third horse was free. It broke into a rough gallop and disappeared into the night behind the others, leaving Jumana alone with the last horse – Nefret.

"It's just me," Jumana whispered to her horse, and ducked under the stretched rope to give her a brief hug. "Hold still now." Nefret nickered softly and Jumana was relieved to hear it. At least Nefret could still acknowledge her. She wasn't that far gone yet. The man had tied the knot quickly and it was easy to loosen. Without looking back, Jumana led Nefret away from the tether rope at a stealthy walk.

"Hey! They're gone! The horses are gone!" The voice rang out behind her and Jumana turned sharply to her right. They needed to get off the escaping horses' trail before the men pursued their mounts. It would be just her luck if they found her and Nefret instead of their own horses. They needed to get away from the oasis and back out on the open desert. She started to run, and for a moment Nefret fought the pressure on the rope, then broke into a trot behind her.

They ran through the well-spaced trees and brush, over small dunes and around rocks, and then they were out on the desert. The men's voices slowly faded behind them until they became only distant shouts and Jumana could barely hear them above the rustling of feet and hooves in the sand. Thank goodness the men's horses had gone completely in the opposite direction. She and Nefret had had that one bit of good fortune anyway.

After ten more minutes of running, Jumana stopped to let Nefret rest. The mare was panting like an overheated dog in the sun. The girl listened for sounds of pursuit as she stroked the mare's neck, trying to calm and comfort her. "Are you okay, beauty? How do you feel?" she murmured into the mare's ear.

95

"Can you keep going? Can you find the man's tracks? We need to pick up his trail again."

Nefret drew in a deep trembling breath, nickered waveringly to Jumana, and stepped out. Despite all she'd seen this night, Jumana was still surprised. Had the mare understood her words? Did she know what Jumana was saying?

Nefret seemed to know exactly where she was going. She jogged across the desert, slowly to be sure, but straight as an arrow. Then a sudden left turn – had she found the man's trail? Was she now following it?

A smile tempted Jumana as she ran beside the mare. She believed Nefret was following the man's tracks. Horses who felt sick, like Nefret did, would be naturally inclined to turn *toward* home, *toward* the place they felt safe, and not away from it, and the only reason she could think that Nefret might turn away from her safe stable was that she was tracking the man's camels.

She still thinks we can succeed, Jumana realized suddenly. *Despite how terrible she feels, she's still trying to do her best. I have to do the same, no matter what.*

The trumpets have ceased. And do you hear that sudden rumble? Perhaps it is the sound of a city, or a vast crowd, or loud, droning machinery.

Slowly, my dears, let us approach slowly. Something is coming into view. A dark seething mass lies before us. What is it?

Oh my! An army!

What rage is in their passionate shout! How they hate and fear us. And do you see, my loves? Behind the army, on that lofty chair – a woman! She is the one we must speak to. She is the master here.

But first we must move through her minions. How relieved I am that we have strength in reserve! I only pray it will be enough.

Come, my friends, we must go forward. Keep close!

Nefret jogged steadily on and on. Jumana ached to tell the mare to slow down but she knew she couldn't, even thought Nefret's neck was wet with sweat and foam, and she was gasping for air. All she could do was run beside her beloved horse, knowing that the faster they ran, the better off they'd possibly be. The sooner they caught up to Bastet's man, the sooner they could turn for home.

If they could catch him at all.

If he gave them the right artifacts.

If... if... if... So many *'ifs'*.

Abdullah's eyes sprung open when his head jerked forward. He'd fallen asleep. Again. But his catnap had done nothing to revive him. Already his eyelids were drooping again. He was so tired! And the rhythmic movement of the camel beneath him didn't help matters much.

If I shut my eyes for a minute, it shouldn't hurt anything, he thought. I just have to be sure not to fall asleep.

And he was flying! For one dreamlike moment he was flying. Then the breath was knocked from his body and he was writhing on the sand as the camel jerked him along. Thank goodness, he'd thought to tie the camel's rope to his arm before he shut his eyes. At least he'd done that right.

When the camels stopped, Abdullah climbed to his feet and gingerly rubbed his arm. His shoulder hurt, but there didn't seem to be any permanent damage. Luck was still with him. With exhausted movements, he asked the camel to kneel. She bleated at him as she dropped to her knees.

"I know, I know," he murmured to the beast. "I'm tired too." He settled on her back, and asked her to rise. The camel didn't move until he insisted she stand, and then she protested loudly before she lurched to her feet.

"Hut, hut!" Abdullah commanded and the two camels broke into a slow trot. "Hut, hut!" They moved only slightly faster. Abdullah balanced on the edge of his seat and peered out over the desert. He would have to stop. He knew that now. The exhaustion he'd felt since passing the oasis was getting worse. If he was going to get home safely, he would have to stop for a while and sleep.

But he couldn't stop just any place. He was so tired that he would sleep far too deeply to hear anyone approach. The location had to be private and secure, away from passers-by, in case anyone else was crazy enough to be out on the desert at night.

He found the perfect spot just a few minutes later. He could hardly believe his luck! The rock field spread in a long finger across his path. He remembered this place. Normally he would wend his way through it to the other side and then ride southeast – but not tonight. He would stay in the rock field and use the boulders to hide himself and his camels.

When he directed the larger camel into the rock field, the one he was leading pulled reluctantly back on the rope. Then when Abdullah finally had the difficult beasts among the jumble of rocks, they insisted on continuing in the direction of home. The man could hardly keep his eyes open, despite his struggle with the obstinate camels. If only he could make them understand they could rest if they'd simply stay within the rock field.

When he finally had them straightened out and swaying along between boulders toward the north, Abdullah drew in a deep sigh. Soon he could sleep. Thank goodness, he'd thought to push the camels' tethers inside their packs at the last minute.

Finally, he felt it was safe to stop. When the second camel had lowered himself to the ground and was unpacked and staked, Abdullah walked to the edge of the rock field and peered out across the desert. He could see nothing in the darkness, but there was safety in that. If he couldn't see anyone coming, they wouldn't see him either. He looked in the direction he'd come. Miles back, poor Bastet was waiting for him, and now she would have to wait a little longer. But what good would he do her if he had an accident and never arrived home? None. He wasn't stopping because he was lazy. He simply had no choice.

He stumbled wearily back to the larger camel's pack and collapsed next to it, then curled up for warmth. Something poked him in the head and Abdullah shifted, groaned, and opened his eyes. What on earth was stabbing him through the pack?

With a deep sigh, he turned onto his other side. The pack was less lumpy here and he closed heavy eyelids gratefully. For a moment, he wished he'd thought to add his bedroll to the camel's pack as well, and then he was fast asleep.

Stand together. We will move through the maelstrom as a packed group, with teeth and hooves ready at our perimeter. We will not attack the soldiers, but will defend ourselves if they attack us.

And my light may be of use. I will give us a luminosity that will frighten the soldiers. Each of us must be sure to touch another in the group, and the light will travel from one of us, to all.

There, see? They stand back at our glowing. Though they roar their indignation, none dare approach us!

And the queen, how angry she appears! Was it a mistake to use the light? Is she now too angry to listen to us, too enraged to show mercy and return us to our own world?

Abdullah was dreaming of a sunny day, a magnificent white
mansion, date palms swaying in neat rows before it, and his
children shrieking with laughter on the lawn in front. His two
sons were running away from their young sister, pretending
to put much effort into their flight. Little Aisha dashed after
them on pudgy legs, and when she caught her oldest brother
he grabbed her, tumbled her to the ground, and tickled her.
Her delighted giggles filled the air.

Abdullah felt a hand on his arm and turned to see his wife
smiling at him. She put her finger to her lips to stop him from
speaking and beckoned to him to turn away from his playing
children. Though theirs was an arranged marriage, he'd
learned to love and respect his wife deeply, and he followed
her gladly.

She led him to a bundle on the ground. Slowly, Abdullah
pulled back the blankets. A child! Another beautiful child! His
heart swelled with warmth and gently he took the babe in his
arms and stroked her cheek with one finger. What would
they name this one? What name could possibly be good
enough for such a lovely child? Something hard poked him in
the neck but he ignored it.

He turned back to call the other children to come meet
their new sister – but something was wrong with the scene.
The children still played, they still laughed and smiled and
ran, but something was different. He watched his oldest son
sweep Aisha off her feet and carry her toward him, his

103

younger brother beside him. Such strong children and so kind! He smiled at his wife. They had a right to be proud.

But what was wrong with the scene? It was bothering him. The thing stabbing him in the neck felt sharper now. He felt the dream slip just a bit.

And in the instant he realized he was dreaming and that something in the real world was actually poking him, he knew what was different in the scene before him. The house was gone. The lawns were gone. The trees. Everything that spoke of riches had faded from the dream. He was what he was in real life, simply a poor man with a poor family.

Abdullah woke with a drowsy exclamation of irritation. If it hadn't been for this lumpy pack, the dream wouldn't have shifted. He raised onto his knees and opened the flap, then blindly rummaged through the pack for the piece that had jabbed at him. There it was! He pulled it out. The onyx horse, the one he'd brought for Aisha. One or another of its sharp hooves had been stabbing him through the canvas sack. Half aware, he slipped the figurine into a pocket and lowered himself again to sleep.

However, he didn't fall asleep again immediately. The dream, the way it changed, bothered him. Was it a dream of the future? Was Abdullah going to lose everything? Would he be rich for a while, but then poor again? He had to know.

There was only one thing he could do, try to return to the dream, and this time, if it came back to him, experience the entire thing without waking. Then he would know what it meant – if it meant anything at all. He sincerely hoped it didn't.

Nefret jogged steadily onward, her head hanging low and her sides heaving. Her pace was so steady and rhythmic that when she suddenly halted, Jumana ran on two or three steps further – and sprawled across a rough stone. Slowly, she pushed herself up with throbbing hands, then sat on the rock. Nefret nickered to her and nuzzled her shoulder. "It's okay, Nefret," Jumana whispered. "I'm not mad at you. I should've been more careful." She felt the wetness of blood on her hands and, taking the bottom of her nightgown, carefully wiped her hands close to the hem. Her mother was going to be upset about the stains. How was she going to explain?

How selfish! Jumana instantly felt ashamed. How could she even think of being reprimanded by her mother at a time like this? She climbed painfully to her feet and felt her nightgown stick to wet knees. Obviously, her stinging knees were bleeding as well. But it couldn't be helped. She turned to Nefret. "Where do we go now, beauty?"

The mare nickered and sniffed the ground. Then she started to weave carefully through the rocky debris – in the wrong direction! Automatically, Jumana pulled back on the rope the man had tied around Nefret's neck. The mare stopped, sighed deeply, and turned to look at her. Though Jumana couldn't see her expression in the night, she could imagine the mare looking at her with exasperated eyes. "Sorry, Nefret," she said sheepishly and loosened the rope. "I do trust you. Really, I do. I'm sorry."

The mare stepped forward again, picking her way through the

rough rocks with surprising stealth and Jumana followed close behind her, holding the rope only to keep it from trailing beneath the mare's hooves. She kept one hand on Nefret's hindquarter, so if the mare stopped, she wouldn't run into her. And Nefret did stop short, after only a few minutes.

Jumana made her way to the mare's head and peered in the direction she was looking. Was the man ahead of her, camping among the boulders and stones? She could see dark lumps ahead but was unable to tell if they were rocks or camels. However, they were too small to be human, of that she was sure. Which meant if the lumps were camels, the man could be anywhere. What if she stepped on him or fell over him? If only he'd thought to start a campfire, then at least she could see.

Nefret reached behind Jumana with her nose and pushed the girl forward. And Jumana didn't stop. She ducked low to the ground, but didn't stop. She knew as well as Nefret that she had to go forward. There was only one way to save the others and she had made the decision hours ago that she was going to try, come what may.

Sobekkare looked down on her soldiers with disgust. What cowards! They backed away from the Enemies like whimpering mongrels. She speared their minds with a single word – "Attack!"

And two soldiers stepped forward from the throng. One yelled and swung his sword at the head of a black Enemy – and was instantly blocked by a shield of light! Shocked, the soldier dropped his sword and leapt away. The second soldier followed, but not quickly enough. A gray Enemy reached out with open mouth and flashing hooves – and the protector stopped it with a motion of her hand.

Interesting! Maybe the protector wasn't a mere servant. Sobekkare watched, intrigued, as the strange golden being stroked the Enemy's neck and leaned forward to speak to it. Could the protector be the master of the Enemies?

It was time to find out.

Queen Sobekkare rose to her feet and stepped majestically forward. "Let them pass safely through to me!" she commanded her army, and with obvious relief, her soldiers parted to create a path to the foot of their queen's throne.

The protector turned to look at Sobekkare, and the queen shuddered in spite of her efforts not to be affected. Even from this distance, she could see the creature's eyes were the color of molten lava.

But she wouldn't let the protector know she was shaken. She wouldn't allow herself to appear weak in front of her troops. With haughty movements, she turned and strode back to her throne, turned, sat, and stared stonily above her enemy's heads as she waited for them to come near.

The dream was back, and Abdullah felt in his heart that it was important, that it was trying to tell him something valuable, even as it unfolded around him. There was his family again, rich and happy, green lawns and mansion behind. His children playing. His mother holding out a plate of sweets to him. His father having a nap in the shade. And beside him, his wife laughing as her fingers danced along the baby's stomach. Infant cooing surrounded them like notes from a magical instrument.

He sat back in his chair. Maybe this time the dream wouldn't shift, the riches wouldn't disappear. He took a deep breath and stretched his arms up. So far, so good.

The first lump Jumana came to was a rock. She leaned against it and tried to make out the features of the two larger shapes in front of her. They could be rocks too, but she didn't think so. They looked too much the same, too rounded, too uniform in size. Then one of the shapes moved. Jumana's breath caught in her throat. Two camels! She'd found Bastet's man! At last!

But where is he? She forced herself to breathe, calm and steady, then slowly crept forward. The smaller of the two camels, the one that had moved, grunted loudly and Jumana cast wild eyes about, searching for human movement. What if the camel woke him up? What would he do if he found her? Certainly not give her the arti-fact or artifacts she needed.

Suddenly Jumana knew for certain what she had to do – she had to take the artifact without waking him. She would steal it, even though it went against her ideas of right and wrong. She couldn't take the chance that he wouldn't give it to her. She couldn't gamble Angelica's and the horses' lives on one man's decision.

As silently as possible, she crept toward the smaller camel. He raised his head and turned his long nose away from her when she reached to stroke his long neck. "Good boy," she whispered, ran her hand down his rough coat, and cast her gaze about for his pack. There it was, that dark lump just a few feet to his right. She patted the camel once more, then moved quietly to the worn canvas bags.

An idea had been growing in Jumana's mind as she followed Nefret through the darkness, and now, finally, she could test her theory. If the object was emitting such an intense power that it was making all the nearby horses sick, shouldn't she too feel *something* when she touched it: an electricity, a strange tension, even a vague unease? She desperately hoped so. It was the only way she could think to identify the artifact.

Her hand ranged through the pack, touching one ancient object after another – and though their textures were different, and their sizes and weights were different, she received the same feeling from them all. They were old beyond measure. They held unbelievable value. But there was nothing evil in them.

Blinking back tears, Jumana withdrew her hand. She closed her eyes and took a deep breath. What if her theory was wrong? What if she'd touched it and hadn't been able to feel its malevolence? What if she wasn't *capable* of identifying the object she needed to find so desperately?

But this was not the time to be slowed by self-doubt. If she checked the second pack and didn't feel anything, she could give in to hopelessness. Until that time, she had to keep going. She wouldn't stop to mourn the loss of her friends yet.

The second camel turned her head to look at Jumana as the girl crept to her side. Jumana was eternally grateful when the camel kept silent. She still didn't know where the man was sleeping, but she knew he could be anywhere in the darkness. She hunkered down by the camel's side and peeked over the hairy body. There was the pack. And something more! Lying on the other side of the camel and leaning on the pack was Bastet's man! And he was moving his head from side to side. As Jumana stared down at him, her heart pounding like mad, he muttered, "No. No. No."

She dropped behind the camel like a stone. Was the man awake? Had he seen her? She bit at her bloody knuckles to stop herself from crying out in fear, and waited for his voice to challenge her. And waited. Waited.

The protector was brave, Sobekkare would give her that much. She strode toward the queen's throne with her head high, and the Enemies, no longer glowing, followed her without hesitation.

When the group cleared Sobekkare's army, the protector slowed her pace. Still Sobekkare studied her. She could see the creature in more detail now that she was closer, and the protector did look tired. There were dark circles under her eyes, and her hair was paler than Sobekkare had first thought, almost white in fact. It looked odd on one so young.

Sobekkare held her hand up when the protector reached the bottom of the stairs and, thank goodness, her personal guards proved braver than the common soldiers. They stepped forward and crossed their lances before the protector, barring her way.

However, the strange girl didn't seem to be intimidated. She looked directly up at the queen and had the audacity to speak without first being spoken to. "Greetings, your Majesty." Sobekkare glared down on her with narrowed eyes. Did this Enemy-friend think she would be acknowledged after this display of boldness? "I have come here to ask you some questions," the creature added rudely. "Will you answer?"

"You have come here because I brought you here and for no other reason!"

"I mean no disrespect, Queen," the protector insolently replied. "However, we wish to know why you have attacked us."

Sobekkare was flabbergasted. How could they not know?

111

But of course they knew! They were only pretending to be innocents. That was part of the evil that belonged to the Enemies, and she would have no deceitfulness here. "Bring her to me!" Two more guards stepped forward to grab the protector. They seized her by her arms and began to force her up the stairs to the throne.

But as Sobekkare watched them approach her, she doubted they were forcing the protector anywhere. She wasn't struggling and seemed to be climbing willingly. Her Enemies weren't trying to free her. Was being seized by the queen's guards part of her wicked plan all along?

Abdullah felt the dream shifting again. The crisp, scented air became warmer. He smelled flatbread baking – the poor man's food. The verdant grasses were fading. The mansion no longer glistened.

"No. No. No!"

Only the faces of his family stayed the same. For that, at least, he was grateful. He dreamt on, and in dreaming, tried to notice a clue, any clue, that could tell him why things were changing. What was going to make him a poor man again? Was someone lurking in the shadows, someone who was going to steal his money? Was the treasure actually valueless, just junk, and he was getting his hopes up for nothing?

"No. No. No!"

He struggled to stay asleep and to be aware of the dream at the same time – and felt only frustration when the struggle itself pushed him even farther into consciousness.

Relax. I have to relax, he realized with his first waking thought. Let the dream happen as it wants. Slowly Abdullah allowed his muscles to soften, his mind to calm.

And he was back again. Dreaming again. Watching his children playing happily in the dirt.

Trying to understand why their riches were fading around them.

Jumana hunched behind the camel, trying to pull courage into her chilled body. Through her fog of fear, she realized the man hadn't seen her. He would have said something more if he had. She listened as he stilled again in his sleep.

Now is the time, she told herself. *Now, before he wakes up for real!* But for some reason, her body didn't want to move. *Just one hand. Move just one hand, and now, two. Okay. Now my feet. Slow now. Slow.*

She crept around the back of the camel, past the man lying just inches away from her, and around the far side of the pack. The camel's eyes watched her suspiciously as she stole along, but the beast didn't move, didn't utter a sound.

On the other side of the canvas pack, Jumana fumbled for the ties to discover they'd already been undone. She slid her hand inside. Swiftly and silently, she touched as many of the hard lumps and edges of the artifacts as she could reach, all the while keeping her eyes locked on the man's face. His mouth was still and his eyes were shut tight, but she could see his wasn't an easy sleep. The meager light of the stars fell on his face, illuminating a creased forehead and tight mouth.

With an effort, Jumana tried to push her fear to the back of her mind. She needed to concentrate on the objects. One by one, she touched them, and with every touch tried to determine if this one was the one. And the answer was always no.

But there's something different about this pack, she thought. *I can feel it. The object must be near.*

"No." The man's voice was sudden and harsh and Jumana gasped. Two pieces of metal clunked together as she jerked her hand from the pack. She cowered back behind the worn canvas. There was another "No," this time softer, sleepier, then silence once again.

The moments ticked by, and slowly Jumana rose to look over the pack. The man was still asleep, though he'd rolled onto his back. His face was in full view, and she knew if he opened his eyes he would see her immediately. But he was still asleep; she had another chance.

She reached her hand under the flap again, her eyes still on the man. And froze. Something was there, in his pocket. She could sense it now that he'd rolled over: a slight, but sinister presence. Jumana couldn't actually see the object in the night and shadows, not with her eyes anyway, but she could *feel* its darkness. Here, finally, was the artifact she was looking for. Here was the vessel that held the poison that was killing her friends! There wasn't one single shred of doubt in her mind.

She looked down at the man's face. He was waking up. In a few seconds, he would open his eyes and see her hovering over him. And the artifact was just a couple of feet away. All she needed to do was reach over the pack and slip it from his pocket. So simple, and yet so dreadfully hard!

"Stop there." The guards stopped, the protector still in their clutches. The queen leaned toward her captive and stared into the amber eyes. "Who are you?" she asked.

"My name is Angelica."

"What are you?"

"I help these, my friends," the strange girl replied.

"So you are their servant," said Queen Sobekkare smugly, satisfied that her first guess had been right.

"In a fashion," the girl replied. "And who are you?"

"What audacity! What impudence, to think you can question me!"

The girl looked at her for a long moment as if trying to understand her words, then closed her strange eyes. Sobekkare held her breath as light wisped from the girl's arms to the guards. Silly smiles slid onto their faces and, seeming only half aware, they dropped their hold on the protector. The girl stepped forward. "If we have been condemned to remain here in this dark kingdom, it is only fair that you tell us why."

The queen stepped back. The protector was getting altogether too close. "You know why."

"No, we do not."

"You do. Now stay back!"

"We do not know," the girl repeated, and stopped a few feet away. When Sobekkare responded by moving even farther away from her, she added, "You hate us, I can see that. But I think it is a hatred born in error. It must be, for there are none more peaceful than these, my friends."

"Peaceful! Peaceful!"

All Sobekkare's nervousness vanished in a flash of rage. "How can you say that! You destroyed me! You stole from me! You massacred my loyal followers and exiled me to live out my life in the wilderness!"

And then, without realizing she was telling the protector exactly what she'd wanted to know, Sobekkare blurted out her entire story.

Helplessly, Abdullah watched his riches fade away, and he could see neither thief nor stranger lurking in the shadows of the dream. The glorious wealth simply disappeared before his eyes, quietly, steadily, irreversibly.

He opened his eyes to see stars above him, the camel on one side, and the pack on the other. He stared into the night, desolate. He was going to lose everything. This treasure would one day be gone and he would be a poor man again. And even though he'd seen no thieves in the dream, that was most likely what would happen to it. It would be stolen.

But forewarned is forearmed, he thought. Maybe someone will try to steal it, but now that I know, I can stop him. I'll make sure the treasure is safe all the time! I'll watch everyone. No one is going to steal my children's future.

With a groan, he rose to his feet. He hadn't had much sleep, but it was enough to keep him going until he reached home. He hoisted the pack onto the camel's back and strapped it into place, then started toward the second camel. He stopped, puzzled, halfway there.

That noise, it sounded like a hoof striking stone. Was someone nearby? He stood still for few moments, straining to listen. He could hear something moving farther away from him. A horse?

He walked toward the camel again, deep in thought. What would bring someone so close this night? Had they been traveling along the rock field, noticed his camp, and turned away?

Or had they been pilfering his treasure?

With a gasp, he ran the last few feet to the camel and dropped down beside the pack, the one he'd left unguarded. Desperately, he searched the load. Had thieves found him already? Was the dream simply trying to warn him of something that was happening even as he dreamt it?

But the pack seemed just as it had when he pulled it from the camel's back. One by one, he removed the objects and counted them. They were all there. And the other pack has to be fine, he thought as he replaced the items. I leaned on it as I slept, and no thief would be that bold!

Quickly, Abdullah hoisted the pack to the second camel's back, strapped it into place, and commanded the camel to rise. He had to get moving again. If the sounds were those of a thief, luckily something had scared him off before he'd stolen anything. For some reason, fortune was continuing to smile on Abdullah, and he wasn't about to push his luck. There would be no more stopping until he had the treasure safely home.

He led the smaller camel toward the larger, then climbed onto the larger camel's back. "Hut! Hut!" He tapped the camel's shoulder with his stick and the beast rose to her feet. She swayed from side to side as she walked between the boulders. Not for the first time, Abdullah wished Bastet was still well and with him. The camels seemed especially slow and cumbersome after riding the quick, lithe mare.

At that moment, he remembered the horse artifact in his pocket, the one that had been jabbing him in the neck. He slipped his hand into his robe pocket to return it to the pack – and found nothing there! He checked another pocket, and another. The artifact was simply gone!

He pulled the camel to an abrupt halt, made her kneel, and leapt from her back. He grabbed the matches from another pocket and hurried back to where he'd slept. There was no point in panicking. The artifact must have slipped from his pocket while he was sleeping.

But impossibly, it wasn't there. Abdullah could find it nowhere on the ground, nowhere between the rocks, nowhere, nowhere, nowhere.

Slowly he straightened and looked in the direction he'd heard the horse earlier. So there had been a thief! And he was mocking Abdullah by stealing the one artifact he had closest to him, probably assuming it was the most valuable! There was no other explanation.

Instantly furious, Abdullah strode toward the camels. Within seconds he was on the camel's back again and pushing them both in the direction the horse had gone. Maybe the thief was on horseback and was therefore faster, but camels could go farther. He'd eventually run the thief down, and he'd take back the valuable icon. There was no way he was about to let this arrogant, cheeky thief get the best of him!

How sad her tale is. She tells me of the Shepherd Kings and of the horrible creatures they brought with them that terrified her soldiers. She speaks of running for her life with a few trusted friends and as many riches as they could smuggle away. She speaks of being forced to live in hidden corners of her own land, a fugitive all of her days.

And then, on her deathbed, she cried out in hatred against the vile creatures, the horses, that she believes were her main aggressors – and in so doing infused a stone horse-shaped statuette with the sickness of her rage.

I must explain to her it was not the horses that stole her land, but the Shepherd Kings. However, I wonder if she will listen?

Jumana led Nefret away from the rocky jumble as quickly as she could. The mare was too tired to move stealthily through the stones anymore, and her hoofbeats seemed far too loud in the stillness. More than anything, Jumana didn't want the man to hear. He would become suspicious if he woke to the noise, and he might even check the packs and his pocket to make sure everything was still there.

When they came to the soft sand again, she broke into a run, tugging on the rope to encourage Nefret to move faster. He wouldn't hear them now, even if the mare galloped at full speed. The thought made Jumana want to cry. The last thing Nefret was able to do right now was gallop. She hardly had the energy to hold her head up, and she was ambling along like a loose-jointed robot. Once again, Jumana could do nothing to help her. All she could do was ask poor Nefret to trot faster, just a little faster. That was where their hope lay now.

And surprisingly, Jumana did have hope again. The right artifact was tied in a cloth around her waist – it was the only artifact with the sickness too, she was sure, because of the ghastly feeling that came from it alone – and she hadn't thought they'd even get that far. In fact, she still could hardly believe she'd done it: leaned over the man's sleeping form and touched the onyx horse's hoof. When she first felt the evil in it she'd jerked her hand away. And yet, even before the feeling faded away, she forced herself to reach out again. Quickly and carefully, breathlessly and painfully, she pulled the dark horse from the man's

124

pocket and wrapped it in a scrap of cloth from his camel's pack.

Now all that remained was to get back to the tomb, find it, open it, put the artifact inside, seal it up, and then hope and pray that the sickness was locked away, that the sickness would disappear. It was still a lot to do, but the end was much closer now, and much, much more possible. *If* she could just keep Nefret moving.

"Come on, beauty," she whispered and pulled again on the rope. Nefret groaned and the sound came as guttural bursts between steps. But she trotted faster. Somehow she found the strength to trot just a shade faster.

Abdullah knew he was close. He could hear the horse panting and groaning as it moved unseen before them.

He tapped the camel on the shoulder with the stick and she picked up speed. Abdullah leaned forward and peered into the night, looking for the shapes he knew would shortly pull from the darkness: the thief and his horse. Within a minute or two, he'd have them.

Sobekkare felt exhausted. Even recounting those terrible years had been harrowing for her. How she longed to be over them. Once she had her revenge, once the world was rid of the Enemy scourge, surely she would be at peace.

"So now you know why I hate them," she said in her coldest voice, motioning to the Enemies standing below.

The protector looked at her with sympathetic eyes. One rainbow tear coursed down her cheek, and then another. She held her hand toward Queen Sobekkare and touched her arm. "I am sorry for your pain," she said in a soft voice.

Sobekkare shrank away from her. Surely the protector should hate her in return, not feel sympathy for her!

"We are all sorry for your pain," the golden creature added.

Sobekkare was almost speechless with rage. How dare the Enemies feel sorry for her! They had caused her pain! "Take her away!" she shrieked to her guards. "I never want to see this... thing... again!" When the guards didn't move, Sobekkare spun toward the protector and said with a voice swollen by hatred, "You will never be free. You and the Enemies you serve will be here forever, either playing my war games or condemned to wander the gray sands! In a thousand years, I will summon you and look again into your eyes, and you will look back at me with hatred then, I promise!"

When the girl merely shook her head Sobekkare lost the last shred of her self-control. "Go now! I banish you!" With a mighty shove, she pushed the protector from the top step, and watched with glee as the creature tumbled down, down to the bottom and finally landed in a crumpled heap at the feet of the evil Enemies.

Jumana stopped. What was that? It was hard to hear anything above the sound of Nefret's harsh breathing, but she was sure there had been a noise. She looked behind the mare but could see nothing in the dark night. Maybe it was simply her imagination. However, now Nefret was looking back too, her ears pricked forward and her head higher than she'd held it for hours. Had she heard something as well?

There, another noise! One loose stone hitting another. Something or someone was coming up behind them, and quickly enough to send small pebbles flying.

Bastet's man! It had to be!

"Come on, beauty," she whispered and pulled on Nefret's rope. The mare moved sluggishly behind her, though still a bit faster than before. For a moment, Jumana was grateful, then her heart sank. She understood what was happening. Nefret was giving the last of her energy, everything she had left in one gallant push.

And it wouldn't be enough. The man and his camels were still gaining on them. Soon he would overtake them.

How cruel life was! To give her hope, to make her think there was still a chance for Angelica and the horses – and then to wrench victory from her grasp and condemn so many beautiful beings to death!

Sobekkare couldn't believe her eyes. The Enemies crowded around their downed servant, lowered their heads, and – was she seeing correctly – were they crying? That's what it looked like, with dark tracks running from their eyes and down their long noses. And, even more amazingly, the protector's hair was turning from white to gold, her skin was losing its deathly pale color. What power these creatures had, even more than she had supposed! Then the protector rose to her feet, perfectly whole, as if she hadn't been thrown down a stairway only moments before.

Sobekkare shrunk back against her throne, panic stricken. She motioned to the guards to grab the protector again, but they were looking at the strange golden girl with wide eyes, and didn't see the queen's movement. She commanded them to stop the oncoming mob in a squeaky tone, but fear made her voice too quiet for them to hear.

Then, to Sobekkare's horror, the protector slowly began to climb the stairs. One by one the Enemies fell in behind her. They were coming for her. They were coming to kill her! And she had no weapon. Her guards were worse than useless. There was nowhere for her to run. No escape. No defense.

All of her life she'd lived in fear and loathing of the Enemies, hiding from them in dark wadis, racing away across deserts, concealing herself in caves, and here in her kingdom she'd thought herself safe from them.

But she was wrong. Terribly, terribly wrong.

130

"Hurry, Nefret, hurry," Jumana gasped and pulled harder on the mare's rope. The horse was breathing so heavily now that the girl didn't know if she could hear her. There was no response to either her tugging or her voice anymore. Nefret was moving as fast as she could, giving Jumana every bit of strength she had left. She couldn't help that it wasn't enough.

A movement caught Jumana's eye and she looked behind the struggling mare to see the forms of camels draw from the night behind her, the man perched stiffly on the lead camel's back. "Stop," he commanded in a ringing voice. "Stop now. You can't get away."

It was over. Just as she'd thought she would, she'd tried and failed. "Whoa, beauty," she murmured to her mare and Nefret came to a trembling stop. Jumana put her arms around the mare's neck and buried her face in the wet mane. "Just rest, Nefret," said Jumana, tears catching in her voice. "There's no more reason to hurry."

The man would take back his artifact now, and all hope would go with it. Angelica and the others were lost forever, and soon Nefret would join them. And tomorrow… Jumana shuddered. She couldn't think of the countless horrors that remained for the world's horses. And all because she'd failed.

"Who are you?" The man sounded sincerely puzzled. He probably wasn't expecting the thief to be a 12-year-old girl.

Jumana looked up at the man with a tear-streaked face. "Please, sir, just let me stay with her until she's gone," she choked out. "Don't take me to the police until after she dies. My heart will break if you make me leave her before then. Please. I don't want her to be alone."

131

It took all of Sobekkare's self control to sit straight on her throne and face the ascending throng as a queen should, with a royal demeanor. When the protector stood before her, she looked directly into the creature's strange golden eyes with as much courage as she could muster, even though she knew she would be struck down any moment.

But then the protector dropped to one knee. "Queen Sobekkare," she said in a musical voice. "We have heard your story. Will you listen to us now?"

Sobekkare didn't know what to say. Were the protector and the Enemies really that ignorant? Didn't they realize she was at their mercy? Her eyes swept over the Enemies. No, they knew. So why were they hesitating? Why were they taking the time to speak to her?

"Will you listen?" the protector repeated.

Still stunned, the queen nodded.

"Thank you." And then the protector went on to say that the Enemies did not steal her land. That they were under the directives of the Shepherd Kings. That it was truly the Shepherd Kings who had stolen her land. That the only reason her soldiers thought the Enemies were warriors was because they'd never seen creatures like them before. Apparently, the Enemies were really called horses, and ate grass, and lived in family groups, and loved their young, and were peaceful, and that many, especially in ancient days, were forced to be the servants of humans, rather than the companions they were meant to be.

And through it all, Sobekkare listened, astonished, that the

132

protector would try to tell her such lies. Did she believe the queen a fool? She must.

Finally, the protector finished her wild account. "I have but two requests of you, and only two," she added. "Now that you know the story, you know how innocent these beings are. First, I ask you to return my friends to their own world, and second, I ask you to stop the sickness." Then the protector stood and moved aside.

Sobekkare flinched back as one of the Enemies stepped toward her, a brown one with long black hair hanging in its eyes. It bowed before the queen and moved on. And right behind it came another, this one black. Then came the gray one the queen had noticed before. Its neck bulged with muscle, and yet it too bowed before her and moved aside. The queen relaxed a bit more on her throne: these Enemies weren't planning to hurt her. Even though they could, they weren't going to.

One by one, they came before her and bowed, until there were only two left – a red brown Enemy and her honey-colored baby. They approached the queen and bowed together – and Sobekkare remembered that she'd wondered about this small one before. It had been so resilient to her hatred. How odd to think this little creature had worried her.

And she felt something else, something she hadn't felt for a long time – shame. She'd attacked the poor thing so viciously. If the Enemies were as peaceful as the protector said they were, she had indeed acted shamefully.

The big Enemy moved away and the small one went to follow it, but before it joined the group, it stopped and looked back. A delightful trilling sound came from its mouth as it turned and stepped cautiously back to the queen. Sobekkare's first instinct was to pull back when the baby reached out with its long nose. She had to force herself to remain regal, remain queenly, seem unafraid and in control. Then the baby Enemy touched her fingers.

The queen's stone face slowly relaxed into a smile. The creature's muzzle was so soft! Warily, she reached up and

133

touched the white spot between its dark eyes. And really, when she wasn't looking at it through eyes of hatred, it was quite pretty. In fact, they were all quite pretty.

Could she be wrong about the Enemies? Maybe they really had been servants of the Shepherd Kings. Maybe she'd been mistaken all this time.

The man looked down on Jumana for what seemed forever. "What are you doing on the desert alone?" he finally blurted out. "Where is your family? Your father? And why did you steal from me?"

"It doesn't matter now anyway," said Jumana, still choked with emotion. "They're all going to die now. I failed them all."

"What are you talking about?"

Jumana looked up at him. "Don't you recognize her condition? Isn't this what happened to your horse?"

The man gasped. "How do you know what happened to her?"

Jumana tried to control her voice. "Because they've been afflicted by a sickness, held in this artifact." She held up the onyx statuette, careful to keep the linen between it and her hand so she wasn't actually touching it. "I've been trying to catch up to you all night, so I can put it back where it belongs." Her voice was dejected, hopeless. The man wasn't going to believe her.

"Who are you?" he asked for the second time.

"No one." Jumana looked down at the ground. "Nobody at all." Now he was going to laugh at her, ridicule her. And she couldn't blame him. Her story was a crazy one, she knew. She heard the man ask his camel to kneel, and then heard his step as he approached her. He would take back the artifact now.

Then a warm cloak was thrown about her shoulders and a canteen full of water was pushed into her hands. "Drink," the man said, his voice brusque. "You must be thirsty."

Tears sprung into Jumana's eyes anew. The last thing she'd expected from this man was kindness!

135

Sobekkare ran the new information through her mind, over and over. And each time she came to the same conclusion. There was no way she could tell which was true: the protector's story, or her own first impression of the Enemies as marauders.

She looked at the protector. What did she say her name was? Angelica? An odd name. Angelica stood with the Enemies… no, the horses, her arms around two of their necks. They all watched the queen with anxious eyes. Only the baby horse still stood beside the queen. "What is her name?" Sobekkare asked Angelica, motioning to the small horse.

"Amala."

The queen smiled and her hand went to the soft wispy hair on the top of the baby's neck. "Amala," she whispered. "I wish you could speak. I wish you could tell me what's true."

The baby looked at her with its large dark eyes, eyes full of trust, and Sobekkare peered into their depths. There were no obvious answers here either. But maybe Amala was offering her something – a way to find the truth? A thrill raced through Sobekkare's body. Yes, the baby was trying to tell her something…

Moments later, the queen looked up. "I am willing to bargain for your freedom," she stated to Angelica and the horses. "But first, you must know there is only one way to stop the sickness now, and I cannot do it. Only you can stop it, though you may already be too late. I can tell you what you must do, and while you attempt it, I can shield you from the destructive power." Then she pulled her gaze back to Amala's dark eyes. "But before we do that," she said, her voice softening. "We strike our bargain."

136

All is gone in a flash of light brighter than anything I have ever known. We are flung far away!

Yet I can still hear her voice in my mind – Sobekkare – explaining the bargain she has struck, not with me, but with Amala.

Oh, my dear, sweet Amala!

Abdullah looked at the sobbing girl and shook his head, sadly. What was a young girl doing wandering about the desert at night? And such fancies in her head – sicknesses and intrigue and death. What a morbid imagination she had. At first her words had given him a start, and her horse had sounded similar to his poor Bastet, but now that he was close to it, the horse didn't look nearly as sick.

He knelt in front of the girl and peered into her face. "Little one, you must listen to me. I am a father and I know how worried your parents will be when they realize you're gone. You do have parents, don't you? A home?"

The girl hiccupped and nodded.

"Do they know you are gone?"

She shook her head. No.

"Then you must ride your horse home, right now. They will be worried when they wake up and find you missing."

"But Nefret… she… she…" The girl dissolved into weeping again.

Abdullah put his arm around her shoulder, but she barely seemed to notice. He turned her around to face her horse. "Stop crying," he said, gently. "She is not as sick as you think. Look at her closely."

The girl took her head out of her hands and looked up to see her mare still breathing heavily, but no more than if she'd galloped a few miles across the desert. "See?" added Abdullah. "She is fine. She only needed a rest."

With a squeal, the girl leapt forward. She flung her arms around the mare's neck and Abdullah's cloak slipped to the ground. "Angelica, you did it! You saved her!" she shrieked.

Slowly, Abdullah picked up his cloak, and straightened. The girl was – how did his father say it – not of this world? Maybe he should escort her home. The dangers about her were very real. What if she'd stumbled onto the oasis? He'd passed close by it and had seen some suspicious looking characters there. What if, in her fanciful mind, the girl had stolen from one of those men instead of him? He certainly couldn't trust her to go home alone, knowing her delusions might bring her back. "Come, let us go," he said. "I can take you back to your home."

"Oh no," she said, turning toward him. Her voice was light with joy. "I'm fine now. I don't need an escort."

"I think I should go with you. To show you the way. You're from the village near the wadi, aren't you?"

"Yes, but I know the way home."

"I will take you anyway, and we must leave soon. We haven't much time before your family awakens. It's almost dawn."

"Nefret is very fast. She'll have me home before they know I'm missing. But the camels…"

Abdullah frowned. What the girl said was true. If he escorted her home, they would travel much slower, especially now that his camels were tired. It would take hours, and by then her parents would surely be out searching for her. But how else could he make sure she'd go straight home?

"Don't you want your artifact back?" the girl asked, interrupting his thoughts. Her horse nickered behind her.

Abdullah recognized the opportunity. "I will make you a bargain. If you promise me you'll return home immediately, and that you'll never wander the desert at night again, I'll let you keep it."

140

"But it's worth lots of money." The girl sounded incredulous. "You can't just give it to me."

"It's worth far less than your life, and that is what you risk when you wander about the wild desert like this, unprotected and alone. Do we have a bargain?"

A pause, then, "Yes."

"And I can trust you to return to your home quickly?"

"I swear," the girl answered fervently. "We'll go as fast as we can."

Abdullah smiled. He believed her. "Okay," he said. "But take the canteen." He held it out to her. "I have another, and you mustn't be on the desert without water."

"Thank you. For everything. I really mean it. Thank you."

He waited until she'd scrambled aboard her horse and said goodbye. Then he waited a little longer, until the horse's form faded into the night. He smiled when he heard the mare leap into a gallop. The girl was right: her horse was fast.

With a sigh, he threw his cloak around his shoulders. What a night it had been! He mounted the camel and patted her on the neck. "Now we go home," he promised both himself and the animals.

And suddenly it came to him – the dream's meaning, as clearly as the water in a crystal pool. Other than the onyx horse, his riches weren't going anywhere. That wasn't what the dream was trying to tell him. No, it was showing him the truly valuable things in his life. Not mansions or riches or green lawns stretching in all directions, but the living beings: the people, the animals. His true treasures were the things that didn't fade in his dream: his children, his wife, his family and friends and animals. And freely giving the artifact to the crazy girl, putting her safety above his desire to be rich, was the catalyst that had enabled him to see the dream's truth.

"And I thank you, little one, for this timely lesson," he whispered after the girl and her horse. The desert was silent now. Abdullah inhaled deeply and thought of Bastet. The girl had been talking nonsense, to be sure, but still the initial similarity in condition between Bastet and the girl's horse was uncanny.

"Now, I'm going crazy too," Abdullah muttered and directed the camel to turn toward home. "There's a reasonable explanation. There has to be. I just don't know what it is, that's all."

And yet wouldn't it be wonderful if Bastet was cured of her sickness? Wouldn't it be amazing to return with the horse master, to find Bastet alive and well?

Bastet, Aswan, you are both well now!

I can feel the others from the village too, in their stables, safe and free of the sickness. Sobekkare has returned us all – all except Amala.

But my dears, do not be sad. Amala herself asked for this favor. Please understand. She asked the queen if she could stay with her and become her horse, not only to free us, but because she felt pity for Sobekkare. She wishes to teach her the way of horses.

And we are not freed yet. When the sun strikes the onyx horse, the sickness will be released from its host, the artifact. Then it can spread on the wind. It will ride on sunbeam and moonbeam to destroy all equine kind. It will be inescapable. There is one way to stop this from happening: return the artifact to Sobekkare's tomb before dawn.

Come, my beauties, let us race to Jumana, and pray that while we were gone she accomplished that which she set forth to do.

Jumana didn't need to push Nefret at all. In fact, the mare seemed to be going much *too* fast now. She raced over the desert as if it were daylight, as if she could see exactly where she was going with every wild leap. Jumana tried to slow her, tried to encourage her to pace herself and make their ride safer, but Nefret simply ignored her and continued her flat-out run. Within mere minutes, they were past the lights of the oasis, and then they ran onward at breakneck speed for what seemed ages.

A shout came from in front of them – Angelica! "Whoa, Nefret," Jumana cried, but the mare was already slowing. And there was Angelica before them, riding Aswan, with Bastet at their side. "You did it! You saved them!" Jumana leapt from Nefret's back and rushed to Aswan's side. "He's alright now. Thank you so much, Angelica!"

"It was not I, Jumana. The queen decided to let us go, that is all."

"The queen? Who's the queen?"

"It will take too long to explain," Angelica said and slid from Aswan's back. "There is much to tell you, but I must do it later." She placed her hands on Bastet's head and lowered her own forehead to touch that of the bay mare's. They stood together for a long moment, and then Angelica turned back to Jumana. "We must hurry back to the tomb with the artifact. If you have it? Do you?"

"Yes, it's here," Jumana said, puzzled. "But why do we still need to return it?" She slid her thumb along the smooth black stone. The evil feeling was gone.

"If it is not back inside the tomb before dawn, the sickness will return," said Angelica. She jumped onto Aswan's back. "We must go."

"But I…"

"Yes?"

"I almost gave it back to Bastet's man," said Jumana, frozen on the spot. "When I saw Nefret was fine, I thought the sickness was gone forever and tried to give it back to him."

"But you did not. Or he did not want it. Am I right?"

Jumana nodded.

"That is the way things work sometimes," said Angelica and shrugged. "Now, let us go."

Within seconds, Jumana was astride Nefret. The fleet mare caught up to the stallion and they ran side-by-side over the sands. It was then that Jumana noticed Bastet wasn't following them. Angelica saw her looking back. "She is returning to her family," she yelled above the sound of thundering hooves.

Jumana nodded. She was glad. Her opinion of Bastet's man had changed completely. Bastet was right. Her man was a very good person.

A movement caught her eye and she looked over to see Angelica pointing at the horizon. The sky was lightening to the east. Soon the first rays would spear the desert sands! She leaned forward over Nefret's plunging shoulders. Somehow they had to go faster.

And somehow both horses did. They whipped over the desert as if the sun was a monster on their tails, running faster and faster, until Jumana was sure they were running faster than any horses had ever run before. It seemed that every stride they took swallowed twice the normal distance. And then they seemed to pick up speed. Jumana looked down in case it was light enough to see the ground whipping by – and gasped. The horses' hooves were glowing in the meager light. And each stride ate up three times what a normal horse could run! Angelica's magic again. It had to be.

She could see the mountains ahead now, swiftly drawing nearer. Three more minutes and they'd be at the wadi, five more minutes and the sun could peek above the mountain and dawn would have arrived – and the horses would fall back into their sickness if they didn't have the artifact inside.

"Faster, Nefret, faster!" she yelled, and Nefret ran faster!

The wadi walls were before them now, beside them now, and now they were past the man's camp, and finally, they were there. The horses slid to a stop and Jumana leapt from Nefret's back, the artifact in her hand. "What do I do now, Angelica?" she asked, her heart and voice racing.

Angelica was already on the ground. "I will return it," she said. Jumana pushed the onyx horse into her hands and Angelica flinched when she touched it. "I can feel its power returning," she whispered. "I must hurry." And then she was running toward the cliff. She tucked the artifact beneath her belt as she ran, and when she reached the rock wall, she didn't hesitate. She climbed.

Jumana looked up at the lightening sky. Equuleus, the foal constellation, was up there somewhere, too dim to see now. *Please, please, hold back the dawn, little foal. Please help Angelica get there in time! Please help the horses!* she prayed, and looked back at the golden haired girl. Unbelievably, Angelica was almost halfway up the cliff now, and still climbing quickly. And Jumana could see that magic was helping her. Both Angelica's hands and feet were glowing as she ascended. Was she making handholds where there were none, and creating footholds as she climbed?

Then three quarters of the way up the cliff, Angelica appeared to vanish into the rock wall. Jumana shook her head. Where had she gone? Had she entered the tomb?

She must have. She must have.

When Abdullah heard a horse whinny behind him, he felt an initial rush of alarm, then realized that he knew that whinny!

"Bastet!" he exclaimed and pulled the camel to a halt. He looked back. The sun was just rising over the desert and the new light brushed against Bastet's mahogany coat, making her glow like a living flame. "Bastet," he repeated in a murmur when the bay mare trotted to him. She touched his leg with her muzzle and nickered.

Abdullah asked the camel to kneel, his eyes round with wonder. She was well! His beautiful Bastet was well! A laugh burst from his lips when he jumped to the sand and took the mare's reins in his hand. Then he threw his arms about her neck. It was a miracle!

Astride Bastet once again, he tugged on the lead camel's rope. She stepped out behind the horse, freely and uncomplaining, now that she'd been relieved of much of her burden. The second camel came close on her heels. Obviously, they wanted to get home too.

Abdullah reached down to stroke his mare's silken neck and whispered, just once more, how overjoyed he was to see her, how happy Aisha would be to have her home.

And he didn't think it one bit strange that Bastet's reappearance made him more awed and grateful than even finding the treasure, for now he knew where his true treasures lay.

A deep rumble came from inside the cliff, and dust erupted from the stone wall. Moments later, Jumana heard violent coughing. Had Angelica sealed the tomb? She watched anxiously as the dust slowly started to settle. Then sunlight struck the wall. Dawn had come. Jumana turned anxiously to the two horses. Nefret looked at her with bright eyes and Aswan stood at attention, his eyes trained on the cliff above. Neither of them looked sick or frightened. Jumana smiled. The sickness truly was gone this time. Angelica had succeeded.

Then she saw the girl, slowly moving down the cliff face. Jumana waited for what seemed an hour at the bottom of the precipice, watching Angelica descend the cliff. She seemed to have used all her energy in climbing up to the tomb and sealing it. And no wonder. It had been a massive undertaking.

Finally, Angelica stood on safe ground. She slumped against the rock wall. "Are you okay?" Jumana whispered, and helped Angelica sit on the ground. The older girl looked terrible – wan and weak. Had the sickness come back to affect only Angelica?

"Just give me a moment to rest," she gasped and reached up with a feeble hand to stroke Aswan's lowered face. "I am tired, that is all."

"I'll get the bedroll Bastet's man left," said Jumana, giving Angelica's shoulder a squeeze. "It'll help you get warm. I'll be back in just a minute."

Angelica nodded and Jumana hurried back the way they'd come. There, there was the pile of gear the man had left. She pulled the bedroll from beneath the canvas and ran back to her companions.

Angelica was already looking better. Her face was a little less pale, and when Jumana draped the blankets around her shoulders the older girl smiled up at her. "Thank you." Even her voice was stronger.

Jumana smiled. "You did it," she said and gazed at Angelica in wonderment.

"*We* did it," corrected Angelica. "None of us could have done it alone. We all needed each other."

"I didn't think we could. It's like a miracle that all the horses are safe." Jumana reached out and touched Nefret's face. It was wet. And so was Aswan's. Did dust get into their eyes? Thankfully most of it had blown away already.

"Jumana, there is something you must know. All did not return."

"What do you mean?" Jumana asked, startled.

"One stayed behind. Amala, Maysa's foal, she stayed with the queen."

"Oh no! What happened?"

"Yes, it is time to answer questions, while we still have a minute or two. Come, sit by me." Angelica patted the ground beside her. "I will tell you of my adventures, then you must tell me yours."

The two rode swiftly back to Jumana's village. Less than an hour had passed since dawn and Jumana knew that her parents were probably waking up now. Soon they would go into her room to wake her, and discover she wasn't there. She had to be back home before then, so they wouldn't worry.

She had her story all figured out. She would tell them that Aswan and Nefret had been freed and that she'd gone after them to bring them home. Everyone would assume someone tried to steal them and failed. From a certain point of view, it was the truth too, if not the complete truth. Sobekkare *had* tried to steal the horses, in a way. Jumana wished she could tell her parents and Amala's owners everything – they would think the thief had succeeded in stealing the foal – but she knew there was no way they'd believe her wild adventures this night. And besides, she'd already promised Angelica she wouldn't tell anyone about her.

When the village came into sight, the horses stopped, and Angelica slid from Aswan's back. She put her forehead to the stallion's, just as she had with Bastet, and closed her eyes for a moment, then pulled away and moved to say goodbye to Nefret. Finally, she looked up at Jumana with glowing eyes. "Will you say farewell in person to the others for me, or to all but Maysa? I will go to her myself."

"I will. I promise."

"And will you accept this gift from me, Jumana?"

Jumana watched as Angelica's hair swirled in a sudden breeze. She reached up and wound a single strand around her finger, and tugged, then cupped the hair in her palm. "Here," she said. "For you."

Jumana gasped. A stunning gold necklace lay in Angelica's palm. "How did you do that?"

Angelica just laughed. "Let me put it around your neck," she said and lifted the necklace. "It represents the bond between us. If you need me, just touch the necklace and call my name. I will hear you and will come." She paused for a moment. "And Jumana, let the necklace remind you to never give up hope, no matter how daunting your task."

Jumana smiled. "I learned that lesson already," she said, and straightened. She tucked the necklace beneath her nightgown and delighted in the warm tingle on her skin. "Thank you so much, Angelica. I wish I had something to give you."

"You have given me a great gift already, Jumana. You have given me life, and all of our horse friends *their* lives as well."

"No, I didn't. *We* did it, remember? That's what you said before."

Angelica laughed again. "Okay, okay. *We* did it."

Goodbye, my dear Maysa. Look for me to come again soon, with news of your lovely Amala. Now that I know the way to Sobekkare's kingdom, I will go visit your foal there. Do not mourn her, my dear. I have no doubt you will see her again. Amala's bargain with Sobekkare was not to stay in the kingdom forever.

I can hear another calling me. I must go, Maysa.

Talent needs me! Something terrible has happened to his girl and he needs my help. I can feel his heart racing! I can hear his hooves pounding the moors! He is beside himself in panic!

I am coming, Talent, I am coming!